James Pattinson is a full-time writer who, after travelling the world, now lives in the remote Norfolk village where he grew up. He has written articles for magazines, short stories and radio features.

# SEA FURY

It was an oddly assorted company of passengers that boarded the S.S. *Chetwynd* in Hong Kong and Singapore to take passage to Fremantle. The old vessel, operated by a line that had a poor reputation, was the kind of ship that could hardly attract the finest of officers or crew and was patronized only by the least demanding or affluent of passengers. In this company, living in such close quarters, there was inevitably a certain amount of friction. But human passions would prove insignificant by comparison when the indescribable fury of the storm hit.

JAMES PATTINSON

◆───────────

# SEA FURY

*Complete and Unabridged*

# ULVERSCROFT
*Leicester*

First published in Great Britain in 2004 by
Robert Hale Limited
London

First Large Print Edition
published 2005
by arrangement with
Robert Hale Limited
London

British Library CIP Data

Pattinson, James, 1915 –
   Sea fury.—Large print ed.—
   Ulverscroft large print series: adventure & suspense
   1. Sea stories
   2. Large type books
   I. Title
   823.9′14 [F]

   ISBN 1–84395–812–0

Published by
F. A. Thorpe (Publishing)
Anstey, Leicestershire

Set by Words & Graphics Ltd.
Anstey, Leicestershire
Printed and bound in Great Britain by
T. J. International Ltd., Padstow, Cornwall

This book is printed on acid-free paper

# Contents

# 1

## East and West

When Nick Holt went up to the boat-deck he found Sydney East and his wife Pearl already there. They were always there at that time in the morning practising their routine. They had an acrobatic and juggling act and called themselves East and West because Mrs. East's maiden name had been West. They had boarded the S.S. *Chetwynd* in Singapore where, so East explained to anyone who was prepared to listen, they had just completed a highly successful engagement. Now they were on their way to further conquests in Australia.

'Always on the move, that's us. Never let the grass grow under our feet. It's a challenge, see? Mind you, we could've made a pile in the Old Country, but that's not our way. Got to see the world and let the world see us.'

East was not in the first flush of youth; the skin of his face, which was long and narrow, had something of the appearance of an old leather glove and his black hair had flecks of grey which he did his best to disguise with

1

applications of dye. He might have been forty-five, but was lean and well muscled, as a man in his line of business had need to be.

Mrs. East was a good deal younger, possibly no more than thirty. She had blonde hair packed in tight curls close to her head, so that from a short distance it looked like a golden helmet, and her face had an immature innocence that was oddly appealing. She was not tall and her figure was a little too thick for perfection, but it was firm and well proportioned. No one could deny — no man certainly — that there was much in Pearl East to attract the eye.

When Holt appeared she was standing on her husband's shoulders and doing something rather intricate with half a dozen wooden rings. East, meanwhile, was keeping four Indian clubs moving. Holt rested his back against one of the starboard lifeboats and watched them.

Nick Holt was twenty-five and had joined the *Chetwynd* in Hong Kong, and the way he had come to be in that colony was somewhat complicated. He had left England with a team of young people who were going to India to do voluntary work. Holt had spent a year in India, digging wells, helping with irrigation schemes, building houses, anything that needed doing; then he and another man named Curtis had decided to widen their horizons. They had travelled overland to Burma and thence to Thailand. They had spent six months in Thailand before getting a passage in a Japanese tramp steamer to the Philippines. In Luzon they had been caught up in a gun fight and Curtis had been killed by a stray bullet.

After that Holt had decided that the Philippines were not for him and had sailed for Hong Kong in another Japanese ship. By this time his money was running pretty low, but he had the good fortune to fall in with an Australian wool merchant who took a liking to him and offered him a job in Perth. The Australian was going on to Tokyo and San Francisco, but he said that if Holt wanted the job he would buy him a steamship ticket to Fremantle and give him a letter of introduction to his partner in Perth. Holt gave the matter two minutes' consideration and decided to accept. Three days later he was walking up the gangway of the S.S. *Chetwynd*.

The *Chetwynd* was a five-thousand-ton steamer that had seen better days. She had been built on the Tyne in 1943 and had crossed the Atlantic many times in convoy. She had been present at the Normandy landings on D-Day and had just returned from a voyage to Russia on V.E. Day. The war

3

over, she had done long and faithful service for her original owners before being sold to a Greek shipping company. The Greek firm had used her for five years and had then disposed of her to her present owners, the Barling-Orient Line, which operated a fleet of similarly ancient vessels, chiefly in the Eastern Hemisphere, and had a name for employing officers and seamen who might have found some difficulty in getting jobs with rather more selective companies.

The *Chetwynd* had accommodation for eight passengers in four double-berth cabins which were not by any standards luxurious. The kind of passengers who travelled in such ships as the *Chetwynd* did not, however, demand or expect luxury; they took what was provided, grumbled perhaps, but did not protest. They knew that complaints would be useless; if you wanted anything better you used some other line — and you paid a proportionately higher price for your passage. People who made use of the Barling-Orient Line were seldom in any position to pay more.

Nick Holt put one hand on the gunwale of the boat and watched East and West going through their routine. East was wearing a pair of cotton shorts and the muscles could be seen moving under his skin; his stomach

4

looked flat and hard. Pearl was in a bikini and as she juggled with the rings Holt caught momentary glimpses of the paler skin of her breasts where the sun-tan ended. The deck heaved gently, but not enough to throw the performers off balance; they anticipated the movement and made instinctive compensation.

When they had finished the act Pearl did a back somersault off East's shoulders and landed lightly on her feet with the funnel of the *Chetwynd* as a kind of scenic backcloth. It was a somewhat grimy backcloth, the green paint with the two pale blue rings and the silver lozenge of the Barling-Orient house being badly disfigured with smoke, and here and there rust pushing up blisters, some of which had streaks of red trailing down from them like a metallic pus.

Holt clapped. Sydney East made a mock bow. Pearl curtsied, her breathing a shade rapid.

'Nice to have an appreciative audience,' East said.

He was sweating lightly; the sun was already hot. He gathered up the Indian clubs and the rings.

Pearl smiled at Holt. 'Our most faithful fan.'

'With the complimentary ticket,' Holt said.

He thought them good. He was not expert enough to see any imperfections.

East flicked sweat from his forehead with his index finger. 'Maybe we ought to pass the hat round.'

There was a smell of drying timber; the deck had been hosed down earlier; crystals of salt could be seen on the bleached boards and the black lines of pitch dividing them. From the open engine-room skylights came another odour — of hot oil; now and then a clanging sound rose from below, as though someone in the depths of the ship were working at an anvil.

'I'd like to see you on the stage,' Holt said; and he meant it. 'I wouldn't object to paying.'

Sydney East tapped the gunwale of the lifeboat lightly with an Indian club; he had hooked the rings over his arm like bangles. 'Some people do. Too many.' He gazed across the awning of the boat at the wide expanse of the Indian Ocean, scarcely ruffled; blue water glittering like a gigantic jewel under the sun. He sounded gloomy, unlike his usual effervescent self. 'It's television that's done it. It killed the music-hall stone dead. Once every town of any size in England had its variety theatre, but not now. People stay at home, look at the box.'

'Is that the real reason why you went abroad?'

East looked at him. Holt could see the wrinkles fanning out from his eyes, the perceptible thinning of the hair. How long, he wondered, could a man go on in that profession which called for split-second timing and instant reflexes? How long before it became physically beyond him?

'Maybe,' East admitted.

'But you were doing all right, weren't you? I've heard you say so.'

East grinned with a hint of wryness. 'Doing well? Oh, yes. We were doing fine. Offers galore. It was just that we needed a change. Be seeing you.'

He walked away aft and disappeared down the ladder to the next deck.

Pearl lingered. Holt wondered how she had come to team up with Sydney East. How did partnerships like that get started? Two entertainers deciding to pool their talents and start a new act, then falling in love and deciding to make it a partnership for life? Or did the falling in love come first? He would have liked to know.

'You look thoughtful, Nick,' Pearl said. 'Something bothering you?'

He grinned. 'Nothing bothering me. I was just wondering.'

'Wondering about what?'

'How an act like yours gets started. I suppose you've always been on the stage?'

'You'd suppose wrong then. I used to be a waitress.'

Holt looked surprised. He could not imagine her carrying round trays, making out bills.

She said, 'You didn't expect that, did you?'

'You'll be telling me next that Syd was a waiter.'

'Oh, no. He's the real thing. He was born in a circus. His father and mother had a dog act.'

'Dog act?'

'Performing dogs. Walking on their hind legs, riding see-saws, jumping through hoops, that sort of thing.'

'Oh, I see.'

Two lascar seamen were doing something with one of the ventilator cowls just abaft the funnel. They were small dark men in faded blue dungarees that hung loosely on their meagre bodies. They seemed to be arguing about the job in hand; their excited voices rose like the chatter of starlings. The serang appeared, a thick-set man with a pockmarked face and a drooping moustache. He settled the argument with a few sharp words. The chattering ceased.

'They're both dead now,' Pearl said. 'According to Syd, it was a good act.'

'You never saw them?'

'No.' She rested her arms on the boat and gazed out to sea as her husband had done. 'How long will it be before we reach Fremantle?'

'Four or five days, I should think. You've got an engagement there?'

'No. No engagement in Fremantle.'

'In Perth perhaps?'

'Nor Perth either.'

'Oh.' He regretted asking. It had perhaps been tactless. He glanced at her profile, at the small, tilted nose, the full lips and the firm, curving line of chin and throat and breast. 'I'm sorry.'

She turned her head and smiled at him, a little sadly, he thought. 'No need to be sorry. Sometimes, Nick, you just travel in hope.'

'Yes,' he said, 'I suppose so. Maybe we're all travelling in hope.'

★ ★ ★

On the bridge of the *Chetwynd* Captain Leach had just joined the third mate, William Finch. As soon as Leach opened his mouth Finch could smell the alcohol on his breath and knew that the Old Man had been

9

drinking again. Finch was not surprised; it was normal. Only if Leach had not been drinking would Finch have remarked the fact and wondered why.

'Good morning, Mr. Finch.'

'Good morning, sir.'

Bartholomew Leach never addressed any of his officers by their first names; he did not believe in such familiarity. Even Mr. Henderson, the chief engineer, with whom he might have been expected to be on terms of more or less equality, was never anything less formal than 'Chief'; but this might have been attributed more to the fact that he detested Henderson than to any other reason. The dislike was mutual, and it would never have occurred to Henderson to call Leach Bart, or even Bartholomew, though often enough in his own mind he did refer to the master of the *Chetwynd* as 'That drunken old swine'. Henderson himself was a strict teetotaller and believed that anyone who allowed intoxicating liquor to pass his lips was on the road to the devil and the torments of hellfire.

Mr. Finch looked a little nervously at Captain Leach; at this time in the morning you never knew what sort of mood he would be in. In a bad mood he could be a scourge to Mr. Finch, who was a thin, nervous young man, almost completely lacking in self-confidence and with a distressing tendency to make mistakes. He had entered the Merchant Service with a head crammed with romantic notions about the sea drawn from tales of Drake and other heroes, and only when fully committed to a maritime career had he realised that it was not at all as he had imagined it to be and that he himself was as little suited to his chosen profession as a tone-deaf man to the trade of piano tuning.

Many times he had vowed to give it up and get a shore job, but always when it came to the point he hesitated to make the change; natural inertia, which was part of his character, kept him chained to a service in which he knew in his heart that he could never be a success. The normal goal of every young Merchant Navy deck officer was a command of his own, but not so with Finch; he knew that such responsibility would be more than he could bear, and the prospect of ever being master of a ship filled him with dismay.

Not that he need have had any fears in that respect, since he was as unlikely to be thrust into such a position of authority as Captain Leach was to give up drinking. Nevertheless, it did worry him.

Leach stared at Finch. This was a habit of

his which the young man found singularly disconcerting. Leach was slightly above average height and of considerably more than average girth; he had a paunch which put Finch in mind of a pregnant woman, and his imagination dredged up the incongruous and faintly obscene picture of Captain Leach giving birth to a child. The desire to laugh made him even more nervous, so that he could not keep his hands from shaking. In order to control them he held them pressed tightly against his thighs and could feel the warmth of flesh through the thin material of the white shorts he was wearing.

Leach regarded him in silence, as though taking a mental inventory of all the weak points of this thing called Finch. Leach's eyes were like large boiled sweets that had been sucked briefly and then rejected; protuberant, watery and bloodshot. Innumerable small veins gave his skin something of the appearance of Gorgonzola cheese; there were hairs growing out of his nostrils and his ears; his chin sagged into flabby bands of flesh that descended to his chest like ocean rollers lazily approaching a shore.

'Have you shaved, Mr. Finch?' Leach demanded at last.

Finch began to stutter, as he always did when particularly nervous. 'Y-y-yes, sir.

12

Th-that is, n-n-not th-this morning.'

'What d'you mean — not this morning? Why in hell not?'

'It d-d-didn't s-s-s-' Finch let out a stream of sibilants, could get no further and decided to try a different route. 'I d-didn't think I n-n-needed one.'

The fact was that Finch had a very weak beard; hair grew on his face in very limited areas, and there only thinly. A shave every other day had always seemed as much as was necessary to keep this wispy growth under control, and Captain Leach had never previously made any complaint about it. Finch supposed that this morning he must be more observant than usual; or simply in a worse temper.

'As long as you continue to serve in my ship, Mr. Finch, you will shave every morning, whether you imagine you need a shave or not. Is that understood?'

'Yes, sir.'

'Remember it then.'

Captain Leach turned away from Finch. He checked the compass reading, scowled at the small, dark, silent man at the wheel, walked out of the wheelhouse on to the starboard wing of the bridge, rested his hands on the bleached teak rail and gazed down at the foredeck, at the battened hatch-covers,

13

the cradled derrick booms, the winches and the bulwarks. His gaze travelled on towards the forecastle and the bows of the ship cleaving a way through the blue water. He had seen it all before, so many times, so many different ships, different oceans. So long, so long; and to what end?

Finch had been correct in surmising that Leach was in a black mood; it had been on him when he had awakened, and the early morning whisky had done nothing to alleviate it. There was nothing unusual about that; he was more often than not in an evil temper. Captain Leach looked upon life with a jaundiced eye and saw in it little that was good.

It had not always been so. Thirty years ago things had been very different. Then he had been a rising young Merchant Navy officer, recently married to a wife in whom, so it seemed to him, were embodied all the virtues. It was the beginning of World War Two, a time of danger and opportunity for men like Bartholomew Leach with ability and ambition; he had his first command before he was thirty. Two years later he had won the D.S.O. and had lost his wife. It was then that he had begun to drink heavily.

Captain Leach glanced at the sky; it was cloudless; there was scarcely any wind. A thousand miles or so to Fremantle; discharge cargo; disembark passengers; take a fresh cargo; back to Singapore, Hong Kong. What a life it was. At his age, with his experience, he should have been commanding a crack liner, not a rusty old rattle-trap like this. If things had not gone wrong . . .

He pushed himself away from the rail, turned and gazed aft along the boat deck. That woman was taking up her usual position near the funnel. Every morning the same place, as if she had staked a claim to it. Attractive woman; too damned attractive maybe; the kind that often spelt trouble.

Gas rumbled in Leach's stomach; it came up sour in his throat, a minor eruption leaving a foul taste in his mouth. He needed another drink. He went back into the wheelhouse, snarled something unintelligible at the inoffensive Mr. Finch and then left the bridge. Finch was glad to see him go.

★ ★ ★

Moira Lycett settled herself in the deckchair that the obsequious oriental steward had placed for her. Mrs. Lycett was wearing a floppy straw hat, a sun-top and white shorts. She had chestnut hair, good legs and a body that was only just beginning to show signs of

15

deterioration. From any distance of more than a foot or two she might have been judged to be still in her twenties. Only if you looked more closely were the tell-tale signs apparent; the puckering at the corners of the eyes, the incipient creases around the throat, the slight coarsening of the skin. Moira Lycett was close to forty and hated the thought; but she was, as Leach had acknowledged in his own mind, still a highly attractive woman. And she was very well aware of the fact.

She had brought with her the usual assortment of accessories: sun-glasses, hand-bag, paperback novel, cigarettes, lighter, cosmetics. She stretched out her legs on the extension of the deckchair and breathed in deeply.

'The air is good mebbe?'

She looked up and was not surprised to see the mate of the *Chetwynd* gazing down at her. By some strange coincidence that recurred each morning, Mr. Johansen always seemed to find it necessary to visit the boat-deck when Moira Lycett was there.

'It's better up here than in the cabin.'

'Sure. Cabins too hot. No air-conditioning. Ship too old.'

Carl Johansen was a Dane, tall and bony and flaxen-haired, with a misleadingly boyish

16

look. There was in fact nothing boyish about Mr. Johansen except that look. He was not even particularly young, having come into the world only a year or two after Moira Lycett. Johansen's trouble was not liquor, though he could drink with the best; it was an evil temper. He had been gaoled for assault in more than one country and once he had half-killed a seaman simply because the man answered him back. Like Bartholomew Leach, though for a different reason, Johansen had found it difficult to get employment with the more selective shipping companies. Finally he too had found his level with the Barling-Orient.

For quite apart from his unpredictable temper, Carl Johansen had another failing: women. At an earlier stage in his career he had been second officer on board a cruise liner which did the Canaries, Bahamas, Caribbean, Rio circuit. Johansen had found that job very much to his taste, but it had come to a sudden and unsavoury termination when one of the passengers complained to the captain that the second officer had seduced his wife.

Johansen had not troubled to deny the charge; it would have been pointless to do so, seeing that the husband had caught him in the act. Johansen could never understand how he had forgotten to lock the cabin door; though even a locked door would scarcely have saved him. There is not as a rule a rear exit from a ship's cabin, and a porthole is a poor substitute for a window as a way of escape for surprised lovers.

That had been the end of cruise liners for him.

Moira Lycett looked up at Johansen, her eyes shielded by the sun-glasses. She understood the Dane very well; she could have made a pretty shrewd guess concerning the thoughts that were passing through his mind as he stood there with one hand resting negligently on the back of the deckchair and his frankly admiring eyes taking in every voluptuous curve of her body. Not that she resented being gazed at in that way. Quite the contrary in fact. She dreaded only the day when men would cease to be attracted, cease to be moved by the desire to possess her. When that day came life would have lost most of its savour.

She liked the look of Johansen; she liked men who were lean and bony. It was Morton's softness that disgusted her, the flabbiness that he had allowed to overtake him. She knew that Johansen was a hard man, mentally as well as physically; she was not misled by the boyish air; there was a steeliness about the pale blue eyes, a hint of ice; and the mouth had a cruel twist. He was, she thought, the kind of man who might beat a woman. She felt a secret thrill of pleasure at the idea of being beaten by Johansen.

'Why do you work on an old ship, Mr. Johansen?'

He grinned. 'Why do you travel in an old ship, Mrs. Lycett?'

'You think perhaps we are both the victims of circumstance?'

'Mebbe so.'

When Moira Lycett looked at Johansen she could imagine what the Vikings must have been like. Give him the right gear and he would not look out of place in a longship, one of those fierce and brutal invaders, leaping ashore with sword and shield to murder and rape and plunder. Again that secret thrill passed along her spine, but she gave no indication that his proximity in any way affected her; she remained outwardly cool, apparently even a little bored. She gave the smallest of yawns, suppressing it with a touch of the fingers on her lips. It did not escape Johansen's notice.

'You find life tedious, Mrs. Lycett?'

She answered lazily: 'You don't have to be so formal. My name is Moira.'

'And mine is Carl.'

'I know. And as to finding life tedious, why yes, I do. What could be more boring than a sea voyage? Each day is just like the last — and the next. The scenery never changes; nothing happens.'

'Sometimes things happen.'

'You mean the ship might hit a reef, spring a leak? That sort of thing.'

'No, Moira, I do not mean that sort of thing. I do not speak of the ship.'

'No? Of what then?'

He moved his right hand a little on the back of the deckchair, closer to her shoulder. His head bent over her and she could see his eyes and the smile curving his mouth, a smile of intimacy, of something shared.

'Things happen to people. When they want them to happen. There is no need to be bored.' He straightened up. 'You understand me?'

'I understand you very well,' she said. 'Oh, yes, Carl, I understand you.'

He began to laugh a little. Moira Lycett also laughed.

★  ★  ★

Morton Lycett was in the lounge playing two-handed pontoon with the Australian, Grade. There were glasses of beer on the

20

table and both men were sweating. Two electric fans made a humming sound but did little to cool the air; they dispersed the cigarette smoke, that was all.

Lycett was a plump, bald-headed man, approaching with no delight in the prospect his fiftieth birthday. He was wearing horn-rimmed glasses because, much to his annoyance, he had discovered that his eyesight was no longer good enough for reading without their aid. His cheeks looked as though they had dropped under their own weight and they hung down on each side of his jaw like the pouches of a hamster. His mouth was small, the lips slightly pouting, and he had a bristling moustache of the military type. His ears were singularly ugly, closely resembling those strange fungoid growths that attach themselves to the trunks of trees. He spoke with the clipped accents of Sandhurst and made short stabbing gestures with a stubby forefinger when emphasising a point.

'Twist.'

Grade turned up the three of diamonds.

'Twist again.'

This time it was the king of hearts. Lycett threw down his cards in disgust.

'Tough luck, Major,' Grade said.

Lycett had never been a major in the

regular army; it was a rank he had held in the R.A.S.C. during the war. But he liked to use it; he felt that it gave him style; there was a certain ring to Major Morton Lycett that plain Mr. Lycett could never have. For a man in his line of business a thing like that could be important.

As to what his line of business was, Lycett avoided giving any precise information; he preferred to drop hints, alluding vaguely to international projects, expanding interests, capital investments, world trade. People were given to understand that he had a finger in quite a number of different pies, that innumerable extremely useful strings were grasped in his capable hands and that a stock market tip from him was as good as money in the bank — always supposing he could be prevailed upon to give such a tip.

'You may wonder,' he had once remarked to Grade, 'why a man in my position should choose to travel in a ship like this.'

'It's cheaper,' Grade said, looking at him from half-closed eyes.

Lycett laughed, cheeks wobbling. 'You really think that consideration swayed me?'

'I wouldn't know, Major.'

'My dear fellow, it'll be a sad day when Morton Lycett has to count the cost of a steamship ticket — or an airline ticket either for that matter. Fact is, I like it. You can keep your Boeings, your crack liners. Give me an old boat like this and I'm happy. A ship like this has character.'

He had almost convinced himself that he really did prefer to travel in ships like the *Chetwynd*. That was the secret of his persuasiveness: he believed in what he was saying — at the time.

Tom Grade was about thirty-five, with hair the colour of a new copper coin, a snub nose and a face entirely covered with freckles. Lycett said it made him feel several degrees hotter just to look at Grade's head; it positively glowed. Grade, like Nick Holt, had joined the ship in Hong Kong. What he had been doing there was even more of a mystery than Lycett's activities. He said he had been looking around, searching for an opening. Lycett would have imagined there were more openings in his native Australia for a man like Grade, and perhaps that was the conclusion he himself had reached, since he was on his way back.

Grade shuffled the cards and dealt. 'You going to Australia on business or pleasure, Major?'

Lycett picked up his cards. 'A little of both perhaps.'

'Looking for room to spread yourself?'

23

'You might say that. I'll buy one.'

Grade handed him the card face downward. 'Maybe I could help. Put you on to something really good. Nickel, should we say?'

Lycett picked up the card, looked at it, looked at Grade. 'That's a very useful mineral.'

'And I've got connections.'

'I'll remember that.'

They played in silence for a while. Then Grade said, 'Mrs. Lycett's on deck, I suppose?'

Lycett answered him offhandedly, 'I imagine so. She likes sitting in the sun.'

'You don't?'

'Frying myself never did appeal to me.'

'Your wife is a very attractive woman, Major.'

'You think so?'

Grade said softly, 'I'm not the only one who does.'

'Anyone in particular you had in mind?' Lycett's tone was still offhand; he seemed only mildly interested. He did not fool Grade.

'Mr. Johansen seems very attentive.'

'The chief officer?'

Grade nodded.

'It's his job to be attentive to passengers. I'll buy another.'

Grade dealt the card. 'Just so long as he doesn't exceed his duties.'

'What exactly do you mean by that?'

'I've heard things about Johansen.'

'Tell me.'

Grade told him. Lycett listened.

'What are you going to do?' Grade asked.

Lycett examined his cards. 'I'll stick.'

# 2

## Forgotten People

Radio Officer Victor Maggs was sitting in the wireless cabin and brooding. Maggs did a good deal of brooding. He brooded on all the things in life that had combined against him from the day of his illegitimate birth to the present time; and these things were innumerable. Always, so it seemed to him, he had been struggling against a malignant fate, with every man's hand turned against him. The chip on Maggs's shoulder was so big that it enveloped him completely in its malevolent shadow.

Maggs was thirty years old and looked ten years older. He had an old man's stoop and his dry, mousy hair was thinning; already there was a bald patch on the crown of his head and an increasing area of bareness at the temples. His face was narrow, the nostrils pinched in, cheeks hollow, jaw pointed; he had the kind of prominent front teeth that give to the owner a rabbity appearance; the skin had a sickly, yellow tinge, and dotted about its surface were a number of unsightly warts.

Maggs was not prepossessing and he knew it. Whenever he looked in a mirror he was reminded of the fact and it seemed only to make him more ill-disposed to a world in which he felt at so great a disadvantage.

He hated the father he had never known and he hated the mother who had given him so little love. He knew that she had never wanted him, that he had simply been a nuisance to her. Even his physical appearance had been a cause for reproach; many a time she had yelled at him, 'Ugh, you ugly little bastard. Get out of my sight; you make me sick.' Perhaps if he had been a handsome boy she might have been more kindly disposed towards him; but was he to blame for his looks? In part he had inherited them from her; in part, no doubt, from the father who had planted the seed and had not stayed to see it germinate. Freda Maggs, a short blonde woman with a voice like a coffee-grinder, had seldom mentioned him. When she had, she had referred to him merely as 'That bloody sailor'. Maggs doubted whether she had ever known his surname.

Well, she was dead now, and good riddance to her. She had never done anything for him; he had had to fight for himself always; and if he had not been a tough as well as an ugly little bastard he would never have got as far as he had. Nobody had ever helped him, that was certain; plenty had tried to hold him back. Even as a qualified wireless operator he had still found difficulty in getting a job. He supposed it was his appearance again; which was all so damned unfair, because he could do the work as well as, if not better than, any of the pretty boys. So in the end it had been the Barling-Orient, and the S.S. *Chetwynd*, with a swine of a captain and a bigger swine of a mate, cramped quarters as hot as hell and radio equipment that might well have come out of the Ark.

Victor Maggs sat with his hands resting on the arms of the wooden chair that was all the seating accommodation there was in the wireless cabin and stared blankly at the apparatus in front of him — dials, plugs, switches, headphones. He had an impulse to take a hammer and smash it all to bits. It was so hot in the cabin; sweat beaded on his forehead and his head throbbed maddeningly. He wondered gloomily whether he had picked up some bug in Singapore and was sickening for a fever. That would be just fine with no doctor on board. There was, of course, that little foreign passenger — Menstein or some such name; he was supposed to be a doctor of some kind. If he was, he did not appear to be a very prosperous one, and he was not the sort of man Maggs would have trusted. With foreigners you never knew where you were. Jewish too, by the look of him. Still, even at that, he might be better than that half-caste steward with the Welsh name, Dai Jones. A couple of aspirins and a black draught, that was Jones's standard remedy. God help any poor devil who broke a leg or developed acute appendicitis; you needed more than aspirins and black draughts for that sort of thing.

Maggs put both hands to his throbbing head and felt blind hatred inside him gnawing like a canker; hatred not for just one person or two but for all the rest of mankind. He felt himself to be one apart, a loner, having no friend in the whole world, nor wanting any. He hated everyone; given the chance he would have destroyed them all, every last one of them. Perhaps only some act of destruction such as that would stop the hammer beating in his head.

★   ★   ★

In their cabin Saul and Sara Menstein were conversing in low tones. It was not that they were afraid of being overheard; there was nothing in their conversation that needed to be kept secret; it was simply that they always did keep their voices low. When you had gone through the kind of experiences that the Mensteins had gone through you no longer raised your voice; you did not assert yourself in any way; if you were struck you did not strike back, for you had learnt that retaliation led only to worse persecution.

Mr. and Mrs. Menstein belonged to a race of people that had known much persecution; over the centuries they had endured it; under kings and emperors, tsars and dictators; in almost every land they had been strangers within the gates, the mistrusted, the envied, the abused, the feared, the spurned, the hated, the tortured, the martyred. When a scapegoat was needed they were there; when money was wanted, from them it was extorted; when a sacrifice was required theirs was the blood that stained the altar. Never fully accepted by the communities in which they lived, they kept to their own ways, their own customs, their own god; and thus they were all the more easily picked out for affliction.

Saul and Sara were born on the same day in the same street in the same town in Poland. Their families were well-to-do, and Saul went to the university in Warsaw and qualified as a doctor of medicine. It had always been understood that he and Sara would marry, and as soon as he had begun to practise the wedding was arranged. It was the summer of 1939; for Poland a time of menace. The happiness of the young couple was all too soon to give way to heart-rending misery.

On the First of September Nazi Germany invaded Poland, and on the Third of September Saul Menstein was conscripted into the hard-pressed Polish Army as a surgeon. He and his wife were not to see each other again for more than six years.

Menstein's military career was brief. By the end of September the war in Poland was over and the bleeding carcase of the country had been ruthlessly carved up between Germany and Russia. Menstein was a prisoner and Sara was on her way to a concentration camp.

In the long years of suffering that were to follow perhaps the hardest thing of all to bear was the utter lack of knowledge each had of the other's fate. Knowing what was happening all over Europe, it was difficult to keep alive the hope that they would ever see each other again. It was a miracle that both survived. Starvation, maltreatment, disease — these were enough to kill thousands even of those who had escaped the ultimate horror of the gas chamber. The Mensteins, with a toughness none would have suspected from their physical appearance, endured all the hardships and were spared the final solution. When the war ended they were both alive, but both ignorant of the whereabouts or even the fate of the other. In the chaos of war's aftermath, the ruined towns, the vast armies of the homeless, another year was to pass before they were reunited.

It was in a camp not far from Essen, a miserable collection of comfortless huts, a place of waning hopes, of shattered lives, of bitter memories. Everywhere Saul Menstein went he saw despair in men's eyes. The war was over but to countless thousands it had brought only another kind of concentration camp.

When Menstein saw his wife he scarcely recognised her. Seven years ago she had been a lively, brilliant girl with a dark, vivid beauty, glowing eyes and a skin like silk. Now she looked twenty years older, her face thin and lined, her hair lifeless, turning grey, gaps in her teeth.

But he knew that time had dealt harshly with him also; from him, as from her, youth had fled all too quickly away, leaving the dry husk of a man. He was no longer the eager young doctor of those early, ecstatic days of married life. But love itself had not died; it had been based on stronger foundations than mere physical attraction. They needed each other now perhaps more than ever.

'We will start a new life,' they said. 'Things will be better now.'

But it was not so easy to start again. Menstein did not know whether it would have been possible to return to Poland; he did not even know that he wished to do so. It was not the Poland of the old days; it was under Communist rule now. He had had no great love for the former régime, but he detested Communism. He discussed the matter with Sara and they decided to try to get to England.

'There are many Poles in England now. We shall be among friends.'

There were, however, difficulties in the way. It was not merely enough to put in an application; there were so many displaced persons trying to get to England; only a proportion could be accepted, and that proportion was distressingly small. The years of waiting began.

Menstein understood that his name had been put on a list. He did not know how long the list was. At first he was hopeful that in a very short while he and Sara would be out of the camp and on their way to England. Later he became less hopeful; life in the camp began to take on the awful appearance of permanence. It was so many years since he had practised medicine that he had fears that all his knowledge, all his skill, might be slipping away.

'We are the forgotten people,' Sara said.

And indeed it seemed so. They were like flotsam that had drifted into a backwater while the great tides of progress rolled on and left them untouched, rotting. In such circumstances it was difficult to keep hope alive. In the early days, in the belief that they would soon go to England, they had learnt to speak English with the help of a Hungarian who had been a teacher of languages. Later these efforts were to seem a mockery.

It was this Hungarian who suggested that they might try to get to Palestine. 'You are Jewish. The Jews are going to make a national home there.'

'But the British allow only a few to enter.'

'There are ways of getting in. Palestine has a sea coast.'

The idea had not occurred to him before, but now it took root in his mind. Yes, that was what they must do; that was surely the answer.

It was not easy; there were many obstacles to overcome, not the least of which was the lack of money: the people who ferried Jews from Europe to the coast of Palestine did not do so for love; they were in it strictly for the profit. Menstein was never quite sure where the money had eventually come from, but he suspected that it had originated as dollars; there were many wealthy Jews in America sympathetic to the cause of Zionism, and there were organisations doing all they could to step up the pace of illegal immigration.

There came a day when the Mensteins found themselves with two or three hundred other Jews of both sexes and all ages from the very young to the very old, herded like cattle in the holds of an ancient steamship of about eight hundred tons. It was a wretched voyage. When the ship approached the coast of Palestine they were not allowed on deck. There were, it was explained, British warships on the lookout for this kind of human smuggling, and a crowd of people lining the bulwarks would have been conspicuous.

The conditions in the holds were unspeakable; sanitary facilities were almost non-existent and the only bedding consisted of a few straw-filled mattresses. The provisions they had had to provide for themselves; many of the people were frail and in poor health; others suffered terribly from seasickness; but all were buoyed up by the prospect of a new life in the land that Jehovah had promised to their forefathers.

They were put ashore from the ship's boats in the early hours of a July morning. The captain of the ship, a bearded and villainous-looking Portuguese, was nervous and anxious to get away out of territorial waters. His nervousness communicated itself to his officers and the motley crew, and they hurried their human cargo into the boats with brutal haste. The immigrants had to wade the last few yards of the way up the beach, but there were men there to help them; they were among friends.

Many of the newcomers wept unashamedly; others knelt down and kissed the sand. All of them felt that they had come home at last.

The Mensteins were soon to discover that it was not exactly a land flowing with milk and honey. They were destitute; their very presence in the country was illegal; and since, in those circumstances, it was impossible for Saul to practise as a doctor, they were dependent on the charity of others.

Moreover, they who had seen so much violence were appalled by the atrocities committed almost daily in the name of Zion by such terrorists as the Stern Gang and others. They desired certainly a country of their own, but not at the cost of so much bloodshed; surely the object could have been achieved by less brutal methods.

But it could not be denied that the brutality paid. The British, sick at last of striving to keep the peace between Arab and Jew, and of being shot in the back by both sides, finally decided to pull out. The new Israel became a fact.

In this young, vigorous state Saul Menstein, after so many years, was again able to practise his profession. Sara bore him a child, a son, and it seemed that at last God was being good to them. They called the child Mark and idolised him. In him lay all their hopes for the future; he would grow up in this new land among his own people, without persecution, without fear.

When the boy was six years old they moved to a village near the Jordanian border. One night a band of guerrillas attacked the village. They threw a bomb into the room where Mark Menstein was sleeping. When Saul and Sara rushed in their adored son was an unrecognisable mass of bloody, mangled flesh.

It was after that that they decided to leave Israel. There was too much violence even now. The country was surrounded by enemies, and every border incident, every bomb outrage, every Israeli counter-blow,

37

served only to remind them of the tragedy that had taken the light out of their lives. An opportunity occurred to Menstein to take up a post in a hospital in Singapore. He discussed the matter with his wife and it seemed good to both of them to get as far as possible from the land that had promised so much but in the end had failed them.

'Very well then,' Menstein said. 'I will accept the appointment.'

He had been working in Singapore for five years when the blow fell. Suddenly, without warning, he was dismissed. It was not because of any fault in his work; the reason was a change of policy in the staffing of the hospital, a decision no longer to employ foreign doctors in that particular capacity. Menstein could perhaps have found another post in Singapore, but, again after consultation with Sara, he decided to move on, to try his fortune in yet another land: Australia.

'Australia needs immigrants. It is a big country. There will be room for us there.'

They were not rich. They took the cheapest means of travel: the S.S. *Chetwynd*.

★  ★  ★

The cabin which the Mensteins occupied measured approximately nine feet by eight.

There were two bunks on one side, one above the other, a porthole opposite the door, a discoloured washbasin with two taps marked, a shade optimistically H and C, a scarred mirror above the basin, and two plywood wardrobes.

The rest of the furniture consisted of a single hard wooden chair and a table that was in fact little more than a narrow shelf hinged to the bulkhead and supported by two collapsible legs.

The paint had originally been white, but it had yellowed with age and there were streaks of reddish rust that seemed to have leaked out from under the heads of the rivets. But to the Mensteins, who had known much worse quarters, this temporary accommodation seemed perfectly acceptable. Even the temperature scarcely affected them; they were both so thin, so desiccated as it were, that no amount of heat could draw another drop of moisture from them.

Sara was brushing her hair, making short, nervous strokes with the brush. The hair was quite grey now and Saul knew that it was not for reasons of vanity that she brushed it; it was a need she felt to be doing something, to find some occupation for her hands.

'You think in Australia we shall be accepted, Saul?'

He stood looking out through the open porthole at the sea and the sky, at the distant, dimly discernible line where the two met. He could detect the faint note of apprehension in her voice, the uncertainty. He hastened to reassure her.

'It is a country that needs people. It cannot do without them.'

'Young people. Perhaps not such as we.'

'Doctors are needed everywhere. And we are not old, Sara, my love.'

'Not old? Not old?'

Something in her voice made him turn. He saw that she had stopped the nervous motions of the brush and was quite still, rigid, staring at the reflection in the glass, the scarred glass that did not flatter, but rather, by its own imperfections, added to those of the person gazing into it.

'Not old?'

He moved away from the porthole and put his hands upon her shoulders. He could feel her shaking slightly; and then in the reflection he could see the tears welling in her eyes. He stroked her hair; he bent and kissed her neck, her cheek, whispering softly to her.

'Do not weep, my dear one. Do not weep, Sara, my heart, my love. I am with you — always.'

He put his arms round her. He held her

until the crisis passed.

'Sometimes,' she whispered, 'I am so afraid.'

'You must not be, Sara. Fear is a thing of the past. You must never be afraid again, for there is nothing more to fear.'

And yet he knew that in his own heart he was afraid also. And would always be.

★　★　★

Moira Lycett stood under the shower, naked except for a polythene cap to protect her hair, and let the salt water trickle down her body. The water was almost tepid, only slightly cooling to the skin; but she felt refreshed by it. The cubicle in which she was standing had iron sides, painted white, and a canvas curtain with rings sliding along a metal rod. She had not bothered to pull the curtains across and she could see the wash-basin on the opposite side of the bathroom and one end of the bath with its heavy, old-fashioned taps and the yellow streaks of rust under them.

She turned off the shower and began to rub her arms with soap. Because of the salt it did not lather easily, but she persevered, soaping herself all over from head to foot, taking a sensuous pleasure in the task. She could still

41

regard her figure with pride. She had always taken a deep interest in her own body, spending much time gazing at the naked reflection of it in mirrors, turning this way and that, bending, stretching, twisting. Like Narcissus, she was to some extent in love with her own image, but unlike Narcissus, she had never shown any inclination to pine away in contemplation of its loveliness. She was fully aware of the attraction it exerted on men; that was the whole point of possessing such a body; if there had been no men to be drawn to it she would no longer have derived the same satisfaction from gazing on its undoubted charms.

When she had finished soaping she turned the shower on again. The sole result was a loud banging in the pipes, a momentary trickle of water, then nothing. Moira Lycett stood with the soap gradually drying on her body and swore at the inanimate shower. It was like everything else in the damned ship; good for nothing, overdue for the scrap-heap. She felt a sudden burning resentment against a fate that had condemned her to a tenth-rate style of living, of which this old rattle-trap of a ship was only the latest and most disgusting example. It was not the kind of life she should have been living; if anyone had been born with a taste for luxury it was undoubtedly she; and the biggest mistake she had ever made had been in believing that Morton Lycett could provide it for her.

Morton! What a swindle he had turned out to be. With his smooth tongue and his polished manner, he had promised so much; and she had been taken in; she had fallen for it all. God, if she could have her time over again things would be different; you bet they would.

She began to wrestle furiously with the obdurate shower. 'Damn you! Work, damn you!'

The wrestling was in vain; there was not even a hammering in the pipes now, not the least trickle of water. Moira Lycett gave up the struggle; she would have to sponge herself down with water from the tap on the wash-basin; there was nothing else for it.

She stepped out from the cubicle and walked across to the basin, the floor of the bathroom feeling gritty under her bare feet. The taps on the wash-basin were of the spring-up type, so that no one could waste fresh water by leaving them turned on. She pressed both of them. There was a gurgling sound like a man being throttled, and that was all. No water.

She tried the taps on the bath. She was no longer expecting any success and she was not surprised. No water there either.

Moira Lycett was furious. She wanted to throw things. There was only the soap. She threw it at the mirror above the wash-basin. It missed and hit the iron bulkhead with a dull thud, then fell to the floor, one corner slightly flattened.

The drying lather gave a sensation of stiffness to Moira Lycett's skin. She picked up a towel and began to rub the soap off, but the operation was not highly successful. When she had finished she felt hotter and dirtier than she had been when she had entered the bathroom. She put on a nylon dressing-gown and slippers, opened the door and stepped out into the alleyway.

As she did so a small, wiry man with ears much too large for his head and dark, greasy hair almost cannoned into her. He was wearing white overalls with black smears of oil on them, and there was a wad of cotton-waste in his right hand, with which he wiped the sweat from his neck as he regarded her with a smirk that she found intensely irritating. It was as though he had some secret, inward joke, known only to himself. His entire expression and manner were sly and insinuating.

'Why, Mrs. Lycett. I beg your pardon, I'm sure. Wasn't expecting anyone to pop out of there. Not just at that moment. Least of all you.'

She recognised him as one of the engineers, a man named Perkins. She had never cared much for the look of him, and now here he was standing squarely in her way, leaving no room to pass in the narrow alleyway.

She answered curtly, 'There is no need to apologise. If you will be good enough to allow me to pass.'

He did not move. He continued to rub his stringy neck with the cotton-waste and to stare at her with that infuriating smirk. He had little beady eyes under practically naked brows, and these eyes flickered upward, as though attracted by something at the top of her head, something amusing, perhaps even ludicrous.

She realised suddenly that she was still wearing the polythene cap, and with a gesture of annoyance she raised her left hand and pulled it off. The dressing-gown was only loosely fastened and the action of removing the bath-cap caused it to fall half open, revealing one richly curved breast and puckered nipple.

Perkins was allowed only a momentary vision of the breast; then Moira Lycett had drawn the dressing-gown over it like a veil and had brushed angrily past him. She did not look back, but above the ceaseless thumping of the ship's engines she believed she could hear Perkins softly chuckling. Moreover, though she could not be certain, she believed also that she heard something remarkably like the smacking of lips.

She felt hot with fury, not simply because a man had seen her in disarray, but because it had been that man; that sly; smirking creature whose mere proximity disgusted her; that man who on more than one occasion had shown unmistakably that he was not indifferent to her; indeed, admired her. Admiration from such a worm as that she felt was an insult rather than a compliment. And that he of all people had seen more than he had any right to see was the limit.

That ridiculous polythene cap too. He had been amused by it; he had even dared to show his amusement. She was so furious that if it had been within her power to strike Perkins dead on the instant she would almost certainly have done so without a qualm.

Perkins, oblivious of the burning anger that he had provoked, went on his way, smiling his secret, inward smile and turning over certain delectable possibilities in his sordid little mind.

Moira Lycett went into the cabin and

slammed the door behind her. Morton was lying on the lower bunk wearing nothing but a pair of cotton underpants. The sight of him did nothing to cool her anger; he looked repulsive in his semi-nudity, his stomach heaving upward like a small, pale hill, a flabby obscenity. And he was lying on her bunk. The upper one was his, but it had been too much bother for him to climb up to it and he had simply flopped down on the other. She could see the sweat trickling down his skin; it would soak into the sheets and she would be nauseated by the smell of it when she wished to sleep.

He noticed her anger. It would have been a very unobservant man who could have failed to do so. 'Something upset you, old girl?'

She hated being called 'old girl'. He was very well aware of the fact but persisted in using the term, perhaps purposely to annoy her.

She looked at him murderously. 'This damned boat.'

'This damned boat?' Lycett reached for a cigarette, lit it, exhaled smoke. 'Any particular grouse this time?'

She took off the dressing-gown and hung it on the hook on the door. 'The shower isn't working. My God, you'd think in this heat they'd at least keep that going.'

'Perhaps they're conserving the water.'

'Salt water! You think there's a shortage of that? We're floating in the stuff, aren't we?'

'At present.'

'At present? Oh, yes, even that might not be permanent. There's probably rust eating holes in the bottom at this very moment.'

'As long as the plates hold together until we reach Fremantle, I'm not worried.'

'I wouldn't count on it.' She pressed the cold tap on the cabin wash-basin. Water gushed out noisily. 'Miracles, miracles.' She filled the basin, dipped a flannel in the water and began to wash the remains of the soap from her skin.

Lycett rolled over on his side in order to watch her, the cigarette held negligently in his small, pouting mouth. The movements of her body as she used the flannel could still excite him after so many years. A professional stripper could not have wriggled and twisted more erotically than she was unconsciously doing in the process of washing herself clean of the soap.

Lycett took the cigarette from his mouth. 'I'll say this for you, old girl — you've still got one hell of a fine figure. You certainly have.'

She seemed to become aware of his scrutiny for the first time. She turned and looked at him with undisguised contempt.

'Which is more than one could say for you.'

He flushed, stung by the retort. 'Perhaps there are others you find more acceptable.'

She did not answer. She merely turned away from him again and continued the interrupted cleansing of her skin.

Lycett pursued the subject. 'I said maybe there are others. Well?'

'I heard you.'

'So?'

'So what?'

'Are there?'

'Work it out for yourself. It was your idea.' She began to dry herself on the towel.

'You're a bitch,' Lycett said.

She ignored the insult. She did not wish to get into a slanging match with Morton; it was too hot. There was an electric fan fixed to the bulkhead above the upper bunk, but it was not working. She moved across the cabin and reached up for the switch. Lycett leaned over and pressed his mouth against her thigh.

'You can stop that,' she said.

'I thought it was an invitation.' His tone held the suggestion of a sneer.

She tried the switch. The fan did not move. She stepped back out of range of Lycett's still questing mouth.

'Now that thing's gone wrong. Can't you do something about it?'

'What do you expect me to do? Mend it? I'm not an electrician.'

'You don't need to tell me that. Can't you complain to someone? It's up to the captain to look after the comfort of passengers surely.'

'I'd say that particular department was the mate's pigeon.' He looked at her slyly. 'Why don't you tell Mr. Johansen about it?'

'Why me?'

'I thought you were on good terms with him. Maybe he'd be more likely to see to it if you asked him. Nicely.'

She had finished drying herself and was dressing. She pulled on a pale blue cotton dress and zipped it up. 'I'm not asking Mr. Johansen or anybody else. I should think you could at least do that.'

'All right,' Lycett said. 'I'll see about it.'

She finished dressing, gave a touch to her hair, then walked to the door and opened it.

'Where are you going now?' Lycett asked.

'For a walk in the park.' She went out of the cabin and closed the door behind her.

'Bitch,' Lycett muttered. He took another cigarette and lit it from the butt of the old one. 'Damned bitch.'

But she was a lovely bitch all the same. And she was still his wife, his and nobody else's. Not Mr. confounded Johansen's, not any

50

other man's aboard this filthy, stinking boat. Only his. They had better remember that. All of them.

He drew smoke into his lungs and watched it drift away from his mouth and spread itself on the underside of the bunk above. A cockroach came out of the woodwork. Lycett watched that too. After a while he stretched out his arm and crushed the cockroach under his thumb. It made a cracking sound and a kind of yellow juice came out of it, as though it had been a ripe fruit. Lycett wiped his thumb on the bedcover and left the pulped remains of the cockroach where they were. Maybe that was how he would deal with anyone who got in his way. Maybe.

The cigarette end glowed as he drew more smoke into his lungs.

# 3

## A Storm Called Jessie

Moira Lycett had been only seventeen when she married Morton. She was the daughter of a solicitor in a small East Anglian town; an only child. The R.A.S.C. unit in which Lycett held his commission happened to be stationed in a camp of Nissen and wooden huts a few miles outside the town shortly after the end of the war in Europe. Major Lycett, still a young man and with only the earliest indications of a tendency to corpulence, was not at all unattractive to women. He had, moreover, a fluent tongue and a way of giving the impression that he had been to public school and Sandhurst.

In fact he had been educated at a secondary school in Birmingham and had at the outbreak of war been working as a junior clerk in the office of a wholesale ironmonger. In the army he had seen his chance to move up in the world. After a year in the ranks he had applied for a commission, had been passed by the selection board and had been sent to an Officer Cadet Training unit in

Wales. There he had begun to shed the last remains of his Birmingham accent and to cultivate the speech style of the upper classes.

It was at a dance in the town's ancient guildhall that he met for the first time the girl who was to become his wife. Moira Heston was scarcely out of adolesence; she was captivated by the dashing young major, while he for his part was attracted by the unstudied charm of this very beautiful girl who so obviously saw him as he wished to appear — gay, brave, handsome, gallant, sophisticated; in fact a perfect cavalier. It was she who made certain that they would see each other again: she invited him to her father's house to meet her parents. With only the smallest hesitation, Lycett accepted.

Mr. Heston was a shrewd man in his early fifties. Lycett sensed at once that this little sharp-eyed lawyer neither liked nor trusted him. Heston asked pointed questions about Lycett's background, his prospects. Lycett aswered evasively and turned on the charm. It did not work with Mr. Heston but it was highly successful with his wife, a fluffy, blonde woman with a ridiculously girlish manner and a high-pitched giggle that obviously grated on her husband's nerves.

Mrs. Heston welcomed Lycett effusively. 'Our dear girl has told us so much about you,

Major. I assure you, you have quite captivated her heart. Now that I have met you I can understand why.'

Heston shook hands without warmth, as though performing an unpleasant duty. Mrs. Heston confided to Lycett later that her husband would of course have been in the Services himself but for his health.

'He has heart trouble. The poor dear man has to be very careful. Such a worry to us all.' She gave a sigh which might or might not have been genuine.

There could, however, be no doubt about the genuineness of Mr. Heston's heart trouble: eight months later it had put him in the grave and possibly altered the entire course of his daughter's future. Had he lived he would almost certainly have refused to give his consent to the marriage that was arranged with scarcely decent haste after the funeral. Mrs. Heston did not refuse her blessing; indeed she went into raptures when Moira told her that Major Lycett had proposed.

'That dear, dear boy. How splendid. There is no one I would rather have for a son-in-law. No one. I am sure you will both be very, very happy.' She dabbed a tear from her eye and gave a little sniff. 'It will be a consolation to me in my bereavement to know that my darling daughter has found such a wonderful husband.'

She herself was not to be a widow for long. Six months after the marriage of Morton and Moira she had become the wife of a recently divorced auctioneer who carried her away to Newmarket and out of the young couple's lives for ever.

The war was over and Lycett was out of the Army. He would have liked to have stayed in, for he delighted in wearing his military uniform with the major's crowns on the shoulders, and the pay was not to be sneered at. Unfortunately, however, he was under something of a cloud. Certain irregularities in mess accounts had come to light, a profitable little fiddle in which Lycett and a certain lieutenant were involved. He avoided a court martial only by refunding some five hundred pounds, which he borrowed from Mrs. Heston on the understanding that the sum would be repaid as soon as he had sold a number of shares that he held in I.C.I. Mrs. Heston might as well have given him the money, for the shares existed only in Lycett's fertile imagination, and she was never to see her five hundred pounds again.

The result of this rather unsavoury business was that Lycett now had no hope of retaining his commission. The army dispensed with his services without regret and he found himself once more a civilian with a young wife whose tastes were as expensive as his own and a mother-in-law from whom, now that she was about to re-marry, he could hope for no further assistance.

From that time forward Lycett had lived more or less on his wits. He dabbled in one thing and another, never holding a steady job, using his charm, his glib tongue and the army background as weapons in the battle for money. To get money he was not above using practically any method, and that he had escaped going to gaol was due as much to good fortune as anything else, for he had been involved in a great variety of rather shady operations. He had steered very close to the line separating legality from illegality but had always got away without any serious collision with the law.

Things had, however, become more and more difficult as he grew older and the personal charm became somewhat tarnished. He had tended to lose his touch also. He had come a cropper on a deal involving surplus army stores and had landed in the bankruptcy court. As an undischarged bankrupt his activities were severely limited; there were too many things he could not do. He decided that the time had come to get out of the country and try his luck overseas.

Unfortunately, he was without funds, and no shipping company was likely to give him a passage for himself and his wife in return for anything as nebulous as a promise to pay when he had made his fortune abroad. In this dilemma he turned, with no great hope, to his mother-in-law.

To his surprise the move proved successful. The auctioneer, when shown Lycett's begging letter, came to the conclusion that the cost of two one-way steamship tickets was a small price to pay for the privilege of being rid of this plausible rogue. He was quite certain that it was only a matter of time before Lycett, if he stayed in England, found himself in the criminal courts. Which would be very unpleasant for anyone related to him, even if only by the ties of marriage.

'So he wants to go to Hong Kong. Best place for him. With any luck he'll stray across the border and be picked up by the Reds. Anyway, he'll be off our backs.'

'So you think I should send him the money?'

'In the circumstances, yes.'

Lycett had picked Hong Kong because the colony seemed to him the most promising area for the exercise of his peculiar talents.

Plenty of Chinese had made themselves a pile, so why not an Englishman? Moira had no confidence at all in his chances of striking it rich anywhere in the world; she was thoroughly disillusioned; but Hong Kong at least offered a change of scenery and she raised no objections to the project.

'It's as good a place as any other, I suppose.'

Moira Lycett's disillusionment had begun very soon after the honeymoon. She had been immature when she married Lycett, but she matured quickly. Long before she was twenty she was perfectly well aware that the real Morton Lycett was something very different from the romantic hero she had, in her early innocence, imagined him to be. From the first there had never been any feeling of security. True, there were periods when the money seemed to be rolling in and they lived in style; but these were always succeeded by bad times, living from hand to mouth in scruffy lodgings, wearing last season's clothes, sometimes even going hungry.

And yet she had stayed with him, though she herself might have found it difficult to say why. It was not that she loved him; indeed she doubted now whether she had ever really done so; she had been infatuated by the mask, but the mask had slipped long ago. Nor

58

was it a sense of loyalty that held her; she owed no loyalty to a man who had so misled her when she had been too young to know any better.

So perhaps it was simply fear; fear of being on her own, of being forced to fend for herself. She had never been trained to earn her own living; she had no skill in shorthand or typing, no particular talents; and though, with her undoubted physical attraction, she should not have found any great difficulty in discovering another man willing to support her, she was too indolent, and indeed lacked the courage, to make the break.

As for going to live with her mother, that was out of the question. It would have been too humiliating, and even if she had suggested such an arrangement she might have met with a rebuff. She had never got on well with her stepfather, and though her mother might possibly have been agreeable, he would undoubtedly have vetoed the suggestion.

Thus, against all the probabilities, she had stayed with Lycett through good times and bad, despising him more and more as he became physically less attractive, and no longer troubling to disguise her contempt.

Lycett, for his part, knew that he needed her. In spite of the contempt, which stung him more than he cared to admit, he had to have her there beside him. In all his uncertainties there had been this one person to whom he could turn, not for advice, nor for help, but simply for a kind of reassurance. Her mere presence was enough to give him that. And physically, of course, he had never ceased to be attracted to her.

Perhaps in his own peculiar way he even loved her.

★　★　★

He lay on the bunk, letting the smoke drift from his mouth and thinking back over the past. He had come a long way from the wholesale ironmonger's office, but whether the journey had been worthwhile was another matter. He had had his successes, but add up the whole account and what did you get? Failure.

There was no blinking the fact: he was a failure. Even Hong Kong, where he had gone with such high hopes, had turned out to be too hard a nut to crack. Those Chinese businessmen were no fools; they knew how to look out for themselves; too true, they did. Eighteen months he had stayed in the colony, scraping up a bit here and there, but never anything really big. It had been time to call it a day and pull out. Hong Kong was too crowded; everyone trying to make a fast million and working all hours to do it. That was the trouble; they were all too much like beavers; they had no time to stop and listen to a man like him. What he needed was a bigger territory, somewhere less cramped, somewhere he could spread himself, make full use of his talents. Australia.

He lit another cigarette and thought about Australia.

Soon he had brought himself to a more hopeful frame of mind. It was ridiculous to think of himself as a failure when there was so much opening out in front of him, so many opportunities. Australia was a big country with infinite opportunities for a man like him. Why, already he had made a start even before getting there. That young fellow, Tom Grade, could be useful; he had an uncle with big mining interests — nickel, so he said. There was a load of money in nickel. He would certainly continue to cultivate Grade, and eventually some of that money might dribble into his own ready pockets.

Lycett wheezed out more smoke and felt decidedly more cheerful. The future was not all black, not by a long chalk.

He was sweating. The cabin was too damned hot. Maybe he had better do something about that fan. One of the engineers would probably be the man to fix it.

He rolled off the bunk and reached for a shirt.

★ ★ ★

Nick Holt was leaning on the rail at the after end of the so-called promenade deck. About all the promenading you could do on board the *Chetwynd* was to walk round and round the accommodation; up the starboard side, cross over, down the port side, cross over again; repeat until tired. Holt had done his stint for the day and was resting. He was indulging in the pleasant pastime of watching other people work.

On the afterdeck half a dozen dark-skinned seamen were busy with chipping hammers and scrapers, cleaning the rust off the winches. Holt wondered why they troubled; there was so much rust on the *Chetwynd* that it would have been a mammoth operation to chip and scrape it all — and then the ship might have fallen apart.

The dungarees of the seamen hung on their small, lean bodies like rags, and the sound of their chipping hammers reached Holt's ears like the pecking of a flock of metal-beaked birds. He could see scales of rust as big as saucers falling to the deck, leaving the ironwork pitted with shallow depressions like so many outsize pockmarks. Two other seamen with paint pots and brushes in their hands, were dabbing the scars with red oxide.

Further aft a T-shaped iron pipe, thrusting up from the poop, belched black smoke. Holt knew that this smoke-pipe came from the crew's galley, and even at that distance he could detect the spicy odour of curry.

Meals for the passengers and officers were prepared in the galley amidships where two Chinese cooks exercised their skill, and at that moment one of them stepped out through a doorway just below where Holt was standing. This was the second cook, a tall, thin young man named Chin Kee. The head cook was older and fatter, with more gold-filled teeth in his head than Holt had ever seen. His name was Min Tung, and when he smiled, which was often, it was like the opening of a treasure chest.

Chin Kee was wearing loose white cotton trousers and a cotton jacket; his feet were bare except for a pair of wooden-soled sandals held by single straps. He was carrying a bucket of garbage in his right hand, and as he walked the sandals made a clicking noise on the iron deck. There was a garbage chute in the bulwarks; Chin Kee tipped the contents of the bucket down the chute and leaned over the side to watch the swill splashing into the sea. Then he put the bucket down, opened his trousers and relieved himself in the scuppers.

Holt wondered whether he was going to have quite such a good appetite for his next meal.

He became aware of someone standing beside him. It was his cabin partner, the Australian. It was apparent that Grade had also seen the cook.

'Not bashful, that boy. Could have been ladies around.'

'Maybe he wouldn't care.'

'Maybe he wouldn't. And maybe it doesn't pay to look too closely at where the chow comes from. I've seen that fat one with the gold-plated smile spitting in the stove. Right between the saucepans. I hope his aim's good.'

'I wish you hadn't told me that,' Holt said. He was going to enjoy his next meal even less.

'It could be the secret of Chinese cooking.'

Holt could never make up his mind whether he liked Grade or not. The Australian was friendly enough, no doubt about that. He was talkative too; but when he talked Nick Holt got the impression that he was keeping something back, that he was not really revealing himself. Still, that was nothing to hold against the man. Why should he open his heart to a chance shipboard acquaintance? The funny thing was, though, that more often than not people did just that. There was something about a ship that seemed to encourage intimacy, an unburdening of the soul.

But Tom Grade was resistant to the influences. In all his talk about almost everything under the sun there was surprisingly little about the man himself. He was like a bystander watching the game of life without being involved; an amusing commentator perhaps, but a little too detached, too cynical, lacking warmth.

Chin Kee fastened his trousers, picked up the empty bucket and walked away from the garbage chute. He glanced up at the promenade deck, saw Holt and Grade watching him, and grinned.

'Vellee nicee day.'

Still grinning, he disappeared through the doorway to the working alleyway.

'And a vellee nicee day to him too,' Grade said. 'Now he can go and clean his fingers in the flied lice and the aplicot flitters. I bet he was born on the Yellow Liver and lan like melly hell when the Leds took over.'

'He's right about the day though. Couldn't ask for anything better. Get a day like this in England and it'd make front page news in the papers.'

'Always get nice days here, chum.'

'No storms?'

'Oh, sure, sometimes. No storms around now though. Look at that sky.'

It certainly looked a fine weather sky; a few high, gauzy feathers of cirrus, like dustings of chalk on a blue page, and the sun as fiery as a blast furnace, slamming its heat down on the ship. From horizon to horizon the sea was empty but for the *Chetwynd*; she was alone in a vast bowl of azure water, sullied only by the black smoke that came now and then from her grimy funnel.

'I wouldn't mind a storm,' Holt said. 'I've never seen a storm at sea. It'd be an experience.'

'You must be joking. In this tub it could be the last experience you ever had. In this world.'

'I'd take the chance.'

Grade looked at him and shook his head sadly. 'You're crazy, chum, plain crazy. Me, I want no storms; just the nice soft air and the calm sea. Let's make Fremantle without trouble, that's all I ask.'

'I'd still like a storm. Not too big.'

'Now there you're handing out a tall order. You want the right size. Trouble is, they aren't made to order. You ask for the small fitting and maybe they send the real big one. And then watch out. One thing you'd better not do.'

'What's that?'

'Whistle.'

'Are you superstitious?'

'Me? No, I'm not, but sailors are. Even that boozy old soak of a captain may be. So if you whistle, don't let anyone hear you. Unless you like being unpopular.'

'I'll remember that,' Holt said.

★   ★   ★

The boozy old soak was in his cabin pouring himself another glass of whisky. The cabin had once been almost luxurious, but that had been a long time ago. Now it gave an impression of shabby gentility; everything a little worn, a little faded, a little knocked about.

There was a settee fixed to one bulkhead, two armchairs, a bookcase, a threadbare carpet on the floor. On a peg hung Captain Leach's oilskin coat and sou'wester; the desk was littered with papers, notebooks, pens, various odds and ends. On it too were

67

Leach's peaked cap and the framed photograph of a young woman. Across one corner of the photograph were written in backward sloping letters the words. 'To dearest Bart with all my love. Eileen.'

Leach raised his glass and looked towards the portrait. 'To you wherever you are.' He drained the glass. 'You bitch.'

The face that gazed silently back at him had a smile on its lips. It was a lovely face, with all the charm of youth and health and high spirits. Leach refilled his glass from the whisky bottle, leaned back in his chair and stared at the smiling, enchanting features that he had last seen in the flesh more than a quarter of a century ago. Sometimes he wondered why he kept the photograph, why he did not destroy it instead of keeping it there to mock him, to remind him every day of what he had lost.

Perhaps it was a form of masochism, this constant laceration, this daily reopening of the old wound that had never been allowed to heal. Again, as so often before, he let his mind slip back over the years to that day in the spring of 1942 when his world had fallen in ruins, never again to be rebuilt.

★ ★ ★

The S.S. *Morgan Hall*, a freighter of some six thousand tons, was carrying a mixed cargo — canned foods, dried egg, medical supplies, barrels of lard, butter, cheese, Spam, a few Douglas 'Bostons' cocooned and lashed on deck. She had loaded in Baltimore and had joined a convoy in Halifax, Nova Scotia. There were forty merchant ships in the convoy, including a dozen tankers, and the escort was made up of two destroyers and four corvettes.

It was to be one of the bad convoys. U-boat attacks began on the sixth day, the day they entered the Black Pit, the region of no air cover. The first ship was sunk just after nightfall, and from that moment it became a running battle between the all too few escort vessels and the wolf pack, with the wolf pack getting the better of the exchange.

On the eleventh day the engines of the *Morgan Hall* broke down. It was at six bells in the forenoon watch, the sky overcast and a bitter wind blowing from the north-east. The sea was the colour of slate except where the wind whipped the crests of the waves into foam. Captain Leach was on the bridge of his ship and he was very tired; he had spent much of the previous five days up there, snatching only an hour or two of sleep now and then, taking his meals in his hand, never getting out of his clothes. He was unshaven; he felt dirty, worn out, aching in every bone and muscle. And now this.

The *Morgan Hall* had been near the head of the convoy in the second column from starboard. As she lost way the other ships passed her by and left her; there was nothing that they could do to help; they had their own problems of survival and the broken-down engines of the *Morgan Hall* were not their concern.

One of the destroyers came abreast and a brief exchange of information took place by way of loud hailer from the warship and megaphone from the merchantman. There was no comfort for young Captain Leach; the escort, having already lost one corvette, could not afford to detach a vessel to nurse the *Morgan Hall*, valuable as her cargo might be.

'I am sorry but you are on your own now. As soon as you have repaired the engines try to catch up. Best of luck to you.'

The destroyer moved away quickly; it was dangerous lying hove-to in those waters and there was other business to attend to. Captain Leach felt very lonely after it had gone. He felt even more lonely when the convoy disappeared from sight over the eastern horizon. For a while the smoke was visible even after the ships had vanished, but soon that faded also and the *Morgan Hall* wallowed helplessly, strangely, even eerily silent now that the engines were no longer beating; only the smack of waves against her side, only the occasional clang of a hammer breaking the brooding quiet.

And in everyone was the feeling that perhaps they were being watched, that somewhere a periscope had broken surface and was lined upon them.

On each wing of the *Morgan Hall*'s bridge was an armoured box with a Lewis gun on a high-angle mounting; in each box was a gunner in a duffel coat. Looking aft from the bridge, Leach could see the Bofors gun on its high, mushroom-like platform, and a little further aft the four-inch breech-loader. All the guns' crews were closed up, waiting. But what could they do against a torpedo?

Leach spoke to the mate, a lean, saturnine man with a slight cast in one eye. 'We're a sitting duck, Andy, a sitting duck.'

Mr. Blyton did not trouble to dispute the statement; it was all too obviously true. 'I wish they'd hurry up with those engines.'

'They'll do the job as quickly as they can. Their lives are at stake too.'

The mate wiped his nose on a very dirty handkerchief and looked gloomy. 'It'll be a hell of a job catching the convoy now, even if

71

they do get them going.'

'We must hope for the best, Andy; we must hope for the best.'

In the event it was not to be a torpedo that sank them but gunfire. A U-boat surfaced fine on the port bow where the four-inch on the poop of the *Morgan Hall* could not be brought to bear. The U-boat's gunnery was good; it was a simple execution. Within half an hour the *Morgan Hall* had gone down and the thirty-two survivors were in the only two lifeboats it had been possible to launch.

The U-boat came alongside and the commander spoke to Captain Leach. He regretted the necessity of sinking his ship; he regretted also the necessity of leaving them in the boats; it was war. Captain Leach thanked him for his regrets. They parted without animosity; at least there had been no atrocities, no machine-gunnings.

The mate was in command of the second boat. In the night they lost contact. Leach was never to see Mr. Blyton again. Nearly a month later a ship's lifeboat was sighted by a Coastal Command 'Sunderland' in the Western Approaches. Captain Leach had sailed his boat some five hundred miles and had lost eight of his sixteen men from starvation and exposure. Two more were to die later but the others survived. Leach was awarded the D.S.O. In a way it was like a mockery.

Leach was tough; he refused to go to hospital; he wanted to get home just as soon as it was possible to do so. His home was at Caversham, just outside Reading, a three-bedroomed house in a pleasant residential area. He was still paying for the house.

He tried several times to get through on the telephone; each time there was no answer. It worried him a little, but he could think of plenty of reasons why Eileen should not be at home. He sent a telegram saying he was coming and caught a night train from Liverpool to London. He arrived in Caversham soon after midday and walked from the bus stop to the house.

There was no front gate; it had been swallowed up by the demand for scrap-iron. There were no gates along the entire length of the road, except an occasional wooden one that had no strategic value. The railing had gone too. Leach was able to step straight off the pavement on to his own gravel drive where the weeds were growing unchecked.

The front door was under a little red-brick porch. He tried it and found that it was locked. He rang the bell. No one came. He went round to the side door, tried that too.

The same result. He peered in through the kitchen window. It was all so familiar: the boiler, the wringer, the sink, the clothes horse; his home. But there was no one in the kitchen. He began to feel vaguely uneasy.

He stepped back from the house and looked up at the bedroom windows. All closed. He was about to go round to the garden and try the french windows when someone said, 'Captain Leach.'

Leach turned in the direction of the voice and saw that it was Mrs. Howlett, the widow who lived in the next house. She was standing in the gap in the privet hedge which separated the two properties. The gap had been there when he and Eileen had moved in and it had seemed unfriendly to propose blocking it up.

Mrs. Howlett was a large, pink-faced woman of forty with peroxide blonde hair. Leach became aware that she was holding a door-key in her hand. He also noticed that she was looking at him with a rather strange expression, half embarrassed, half compassionate.

'You're thinner,' she said. 'Have you been ill?'

'Not ill,' Leach said. 'Is that my key?'

She handed it to him, still with that same embarrassed, compassionate expression that he could not, or did not wish, to understand. 'Eileen asked me to give it to you when you came.'

'Thank you,' he said.

It was the key to the front door. He let himself in and the chill of the house struck him at once. It seemed to send a chill into his heart.

The envelope was propped up on the table in the sitting-room; the gate-legged table that they had bought in a sale in Reading. The envelope bore one word in Eileen's backward sloping handwriting: 'Bart'.

He hesitated before opening it, having a presentiment of what it might contain. Then he slit the flap and took out the single sheet of writing paper that was inside.

The message was brief to the point of brutality. But perhaps, if such a message had to be written, that was the best way, since no amount of dressing it up in sugared words could have made it less bitter.

'Bart Dear. I have fallen in love with another man. Really in love this time. I realise now that marrying you was a terrible mistake. This will be a shock to you, I know, but you will get over it. One gets over everything . . . '

One gets over everything! Even an incurable disease? Yes — in the grave. He would as soon get over the memory of her. As long as life lasted he knew that she would be in his mind, the wound in his heart.

And the irony of it was that it was she who had kept him alive through the ordeal in the Atlantic. The thought of her had sustained him when he might otherwise have given up the struggle. And perhaps at the very time when her image had been in his mind, urging him to endure for her sake if for nothing else, she herself had been in the arms of this other man, making love, laughing; laughing at him, the fool, the cuckold.

With a gesture of anger he crushed the letter in his hand and threw it away. If only he could as easily have thrown away the memory!

That night he went out and got drunk. Whisky was hard to find but he managed to buy a bottle. He drank it all and woke up next morning with a mouth like sand, a throbbing head and the agony of his loneliness. He had been hitting the bottle ever since, trying to forget and yet knowing that he could never do so; indeed not truly desiring forgetfulness.

His attitude to the woman who had been his wife was a strange mixture of love and hate; it was something that affected his whole life. Some men would have been able to get the sickness out of their systems and start afresh. But not Leach; just as he had kept her picture, so he had kept the memory like a brand burned in his flesh, and no day passed without bringing the bitter thought of that betrayal back into his twisted mind.

★ ★ ★

Leach raised the glass to his lips and poured the whisky down his throat. He felt the liquid fire of the spirit flaming through his blood and it roused him to sudden fury. With a jerk of his arm he flung the empty glass at the photograph of the smiling girl on his desk. The glass missed the target, broke against the back of the desk and fell in fragments. He seized the whisky bottle and flung that also. It, too, missed the photograph, broke on the desk and fell among the papers in a shower of glass and liquor.

Goaded to even blinder fury by the failure of his aim, Leach pushed himself up from the chair, lurched to the desk and grabbed the photograph-frame with his right hand. He threw it to the floor and jumped on it, dancing up and down, grinding it underfoot.

'Bitch! Whore! Jezebel!'

His face was contorted, his eyes staring;

saliva dribbled from his mouth as he spat out the words.

It was thus that Maggs, the radio officer, had the ill fortune to surprise him. The moment could not have been more badly chosen.

Maggs had knocked twice before entering and then had misconstrued the muffled words coming through the door as an invitation to walk in. Maggs walked in to find Leach in the middle of his dance of hate. He stopped dead just inside the cabin and stared in amazement at the spectacle of the master of the *Chetwynd* behaving as though demented. His immediate impulse was to retire at once, but a kind of awed fascination held him there, gazing in wonder at this remarkable exhibition.

Leach continued with his leaping and stamping, his mouthing of words of hatred, for perhaps half a minute before he noticed Maggs. When his eyes did light on the radio officer he stopped immediately. He was not so demented that he failed to realise how ridiculous he was making himself. And in front of this wretched apology for a man of all people. His fury, deflected from the photograph, vented itself instead on the unfortunate Maggs.

'Damn you, Sparks! What in hell d'you

mean by bursting in here like that? Where are your manners, man? Or is it too much to expect manners in a product of the back streets and the gutter?'

Maggs turned white. He was not to know that any other man standing in that particular place at that particular time would have received exactly the same kind of greeting. Sensitive as he was in the matter of his birth and upbringing, the remark cut deeply. He began to tremble. He trembled because he had an almost irresistible impulse to hit Captain Leach right in his filthy, insulting, saliva-dripping mouth. And he knew that if he did that the consequences for him might be very unpleasant indeed.

'Well?' Leach demanded. 'What do you want? Why don't you say something? Why are you standing there like a dumb bloody bastard?'

Again, by mischance, he had found just the word most nicely calculated to touch on Maggs's sensitive spot. Knowing himself to be illegitimate, he took the word in its literal meaning and resented it all the more bitterly for the fact that it happened to be an accurate description. Maggs would never have told a man to smile when he called him that, since to him it was an unacceptable insult whether offered with a smile or with a scowl. He had turned pale at first; now the blood rushed to his face, making it glow all over as though it had been scorched with fire.

Leach glowered at his silent radio officer, growing more and more angered by the man's silence, which seemed to him very much like dumb insolence. He shifted his feet and the broken glass of the picture-frame grated harshly under the soles of his shoes.

'Well, out with it, can't you? You've got a tongue, for God's sake. What do you want?'

Maggs licked his dry lips and felt venomous. 'Nothing,' he muttered. 'Nothing.'

Leach glared at him. 'Nothing? Then why come in here? You can't have come for nothing.'

'A mistake.'

'A mistake!' Leach's voice rose in anger. 'You push your way in here without so much as a knock on the door and then you have the infernal impudence to call it a mistake!'

'I did knock.'

'You're a bloody liar.'

'I knocked twice. Perhaps you were too busy to hear.' Maggs had not bothered to keep the sneer out of his voice 'You seemed to be busy.'

Leach glanced at the photograph and wrecked frame lying under his feet. He glanced at the broken glass on the desk, at the whisky dripping to the floor. His gaze switched back to Maggs and he detected, or thought he detected, a twist to the little man's ugly mouth that might have been a grin. Mockery from such a man! Leach's fury rose to boiling-point. He took a step towards Maggs and swung a clenched fist. Maggs ducked, but not quickly enough. Leach's fist struck his head, slamming him back against the door.

'Get to hell out of here,' Leach snarled. 'Go back to your bloody hole, you weasel.'

Maggs was hurt. A blow from Leach's fist was no light matter. But it was not the physical injury that he felt most; it was the indignity of it. All right then; if that was the way he was to be treated, all right. To the devil with Leach; to the devil with the whole flaming lot of them. Let them take what was coming to them and see how they liked it. Maybe that would teach them not to be so high and mighty. Yes, you bet it would.

Without another glance at Leach he turned and walked out of the cabin. He went up on deck and crossed to the port rails. From his pocket he took a sheet of flimsy paper, rolled it into a tight ball and flung it into the sea.

He watched it floating away on the surface of the water, a tiny atom in a waste of ocean.

He watched it until he could see it no more. Then he turned away from the rails with a feeling of exultation, a kind of power. He felt as though he held the lives of all the people in the ship in the hollow of his own small hand.

Only he knew that on the paper that he had just tossed overboard was a signal that had come through on the radio, a warning concerning a storm called Jessie. It was the kind of storm that had different names in different parts of the world: in the West Indies and the United States it was a hurricane; in the Bay of Bengal and the Arabian Sea it was a cyclone; in the China Sea it was a typhoon; while in the waters in which the *Chetwynd* was then steaming it was known by the aboriginal name of willy-willy. If the ship stayed on her present course and if Jessie also moved as predicted by the weather men it was almost inevitable that sooner or later the two would meet, since their paths were slowly converging like the two sides of a triangle.

For the *Chetwynd* such a meeting was likely to prove at best a highly unpleasant experience, at worst disastrous.

The chip on Maggs's shoulder was now so heavy that he could even contemplate with equanimity his own involvement in that possible disaster if only it might be the means of taking his revenge on Captain Leach.

Maggs, without doubt, was more than a little mad.

# 4

## Ah Mai

Sydney East was exercising his fingers on a rubber ball, squeezing it, allowing it to expand again. In his business you had to keep the fingers strong and supple.

Pearl was sewing a button on one of his shirts; the female half even of an acrobatic and juggling team had to turn her hand to domestic tasks, especially when the team was not terribly prosperous.

She said, not lifting her eyes from the sewing, voicing that uneasiness concerning the future which she could never banish completely from her mind, 'Do you really think it will work out, Syd?'

He went on squeezing the ball, his fingers pressing and relaxing, pressing and relaxing, again and again. He was standing with his back to her, looking out through the porthole, watching the glitter of the sunlight reflected in the sea.

'Do I think what will work out?'

Though he asked the question, he knew what she meant; only too well, he knew. And it worried him a little also, though he never admitted it.

'You know. Australia. Will there be anything for us there? Will there?'

He did not turn. She severed the cotton with her teeth and looked at his strong back, at the muscular shape of his neck that she knew so well. She was worried for him more than for herself; she could always find something to do; if it came to the worst she could go back to the old kind of job, become a waitress again.

But Syd was different; the world of show business had been his world from childhood; it was everything to him. Whenever she suggested that there might be other ways of earning a living, easier, safer ways, he would dismiss the idea with contempt.

'You expect me to work in an office or something? Me, Sydney East? You must be out of your mind.'

It was useless to point out that it did not have to be an office job, that there were plenty of other openings for a man of his age and ability. But it might not always be so; he was not getting any younger; if he were going to make the break now surely was the time. But would he? Would he not go on trying to fight his way back to the top even though he must surely realise the attempt was doomed to failure?

'Of course there'll be something for us,' he said. 'It's a big country, Australia. Growing fast. New people pouring in. People need entertaining, don't they? They don't work all the time. They've got to have relaxation.'

'They've got television.'

Television was the villain of the piece. It was television that Sydney East always blamed for the death of the music-halls, the provincial theatre circuits. Pearl believed they would have died anyway; television just gave them the final push. But it was no use telling him that.

Now he switched his ground. 'Why shouldn't we get on television? The telly has to have entertainers too, you know. Somebody has to get up in front of the cameras and perform.'

It was an old dream. He had dreamed about it in England too, but it had never come to anything. The competition was too fierce. And why would it be any easier in Australia? She wished he would come to terms with the situation, stop dreaming about impossible successes; that way there could lie nothing but disappointment. She was woman enough to hanker after security, and she could see no security in the East and West line of country.

East pursued the subject; he turned away from the porthole and faced his wife; he even stopped squeezing the ball. 'If we could just get a chance on Australian television it might be the start of something really big. Millions see you. Maybe they like you. They want more.'

She could see that light in his eyes that she knew only too well and had learnt to distrust. It was his visionary look. But what could there be for them on Australian television? Most of the programmes were probably canned imports from the United States or Britain. Australian performers emigrated, didn't they? So what hope was there for newcomers? She wanted to tell him not to kid himself; that it was all wishful thinking and would never come to anything; but she could not bring herself to damp his enthusiasm.

And perhaps there was no need for her to do so; perhaps he realised that it was just a pipe-dream, for the light in his eyes faded and he threw the ball away with a gesture that had about it a certain hint of defeat. He gave a laugh, but there was more of bitterness in the sound than gaiety.

'Ah, why worry our heads about all that anyway? We're not there yet.'

He looked at himself in the mirror above the wash-basin and pushed his fingers through his hair. Not as much of it to resist the combing fingers as there had once been, and those flecks of grey were showing through again. Yet he was not old, not yet, not by a long chalk. A few years older than he had been when he had teamed up with Pearl though; no denying that. He grinned suddenly, recalling their first meeting; the memory never failed to bring a warm glow into his heart.

'Remember that day, honey?' He always used that American term of endearment. It seemed to be so right for her.

She liked to hear him call her that. She knew the day he meant too; there was no need to ask that.

'It was raining.'

★　★　★

Of course it was raining; it was one of those wet summers. The beach was practically deserted and you could see the deckchairs flapping damply in the wind. There were boats pulled up on the sand, the rain beating against their sides and dripping down the boards. Nobody wanted to go for a sea trip on a day like that.

He was feeling cold and miserable. Three days ago Shirley had taken a powder, gone off with some man who had been down there on holiday and had seen her on the stage at the Pavilion. Shirley was not irreplaceable; she had very little talent for anything except looking sexy in tights and spangles; but it had made things awkward. He had to get one of the chorus girls to fill in; all she had to do was hand him things, but some girls couldn't even do that without dropping them and getting a laugh in the wrong place. It made him edgy and he was not giving of his best; he knew that. The manager of the Pavilion knew it too, and remarked on it. Which was not the kind of remark Sydney East liked to hear.

He went into a little café just off the sea front, one he had never been in before. It was a slack time and there were only half a dozen other customers. They all looked depressed, and maybe that was what made the waitress who came to take his order seem such a contrast. He would have expected her to be depressed too; after all, it was not much of a job, carrying trays of food round all day, being at everyone's beck and call, picking up threepenny tips under plates. But, amazingly, she looked as bright and cheerful as if she had been doing something as enjoyable as roller-skating or taking a ride on the scenic railway.

It was her cheerfulness that induced him to

strike up a conversation; that and the fact that she was very pleasant to look at. She was easy to talk to; in two minutes he had found out that her name was Pearl West.

'Well, now, that's a coincidence,' he said. 'I'm Sydney East.'

She smiled, and it was the most enchanting smile he had ever seen, and utterly without guile. 'I know. I've seen you on the stage.'

He discovered that she had in fact seen him more than once and that she thought his act wonderful. 'I don't know how you do it, Mr. East; I really don't.'

'It's practice.'

'But you must have a gift.'

'Well, yes,' he admitted, 'it's got to be in you.'

'I could never do anything like that.'

He looked at her, and already the idea was taking form in his mind. She had the figure; a little too plump perhaps, but it would soon fine down; and she had the face of an angel.

'You never know till you try.'

But he said nothing more at that time; he was not the man to go at things blindly. Nevertheless, the name seemed like an omen. He could picture the billing with his mind's eye: East and West. It had a ring to it.

A ring in more senses than one, because by the time he had made up his mind to suggest that she should become his partner on the stage he had already fallen in love with her and wanted her as his partner for life. Three weeks later they were married. A comedian named Hector Hanbury, who was billed as Hilarious Hector (Has Them In Hysterics), was best man and the manager of the Pavilion condescended to give the bride away, seeing that she had been brought up by Dr. Barnardo's and had no known relatives.

Sydney East had never regretted taking this momentous step. He would have married Pearl even if she had been quite useless from the theatrical angle; the fact that she took to the business as if born into it was just a bonus, and a very useful bonus at that. Soon she was doing far more than hand him the apparatus and look decorative; she was really part of the act. East and West had arrived.

The years that followed were the good years. East and West were in demand; there were long runs in pantomime, good seaside engagements for the summer months, provincial theatre bookings; never top of the bill but not in the worst position either. There was money in the bank. He even bought a car, which made travelling easier.

Then things started to go wrong. He twisted an arm and was out of action for several months. After that engagements were somehow not so good and became less and less easy to get. They spent more time 'resting'; the bank balance dwindled; the car had to be sold. The circuits were shrinking as more and more theatres closed their doors.

It was the time of the nude shows, a last desperate attempt to keep the music-hall going; but it was not the same music-hall any more and the audiences were different; mostly male, mostly there for the erotic part of the bill, unappreciative of real talent, even derisive. Playing to a house like that could be sheer hell; there was none of the old rapport between performer and audience, none of the elation when applause came for a particularly difficult feat. Too often there was no applause at all; just a chilly silence that was like ice in the heart.

The true performers no longer headed the bills; the real attractions were Les Nudes, Les Girls, Les Lovelies. Sydney East could remember one occasion when an entertainer who did a kind of Fred Astaire turn and called himself Les Legs went on in a grubby little North Country theatre. He was practically hooted off by a disappointed audience that had been expecting something altogether different. It was the day of the strippers and the blue jokes, and real artistry was at a discount.

But even the nude shows failed to save the music-hall. The strippers went into the more intimate atmosphere of the clubs and the theatres continued to close down or become bingo halls. East and West did more resting than work, and it was no longer a case of picking and choosing engagements; you had to take what was offered, even if it was a pretty miserable offer at that, even if, in the last resort, it carried you off with a strange, mixed company to parts of the world as distant as Malaysia, to makeshift theatres in out-of-the-way towns and villages, finally to Singapore and the decision to try Australia.

It could scarcely be worse there. It might be a great deal better. It had to be.

★ ★ ★

'There's an alternative, you know,' Pearl said.

He glanced at her, wondering what she was talking about. He had been lost in his memories. 'Alternative to what?'

She answered without looking at him, as if nervous of meeting his eyes. 'To East and West.'

'I don't get you. Do you mean change the name of the act? How would that help?'

'I mean drop the act altogether.'

So she was on to that again. She wanted

him to get a job. Him. 'You're crazy.'

'I think we're finished, Syd. It's time we faced the facts. Things are never going to get any better.'

'We'd be finished if we dropped the act. It's all we have.'

'No, Syd, not all.'

'You tell me what else then. Go on, tell me. Money in the bank? An estate to retire to?'

'I'm not talking about retirement.'

'Then what are you talking about?'

She faced him now, not flinching. 'About you getting a job, Syd.'

He made a gesture of impatience. 'I knew we'd get round to that. I knew that was coming. I thought we'd settled that once and for all.'

'I wish you'd change your mind.'

'Then you can go on wishing.' He was angry and his voice had grown harsh. 'And you'll be wasting your time because that's one wish that's never coming true. Never.'

She did not attempt to plead with him. She just gave a sigh. He saw the way her shoulders drooped and was sorry for having lashed at her with his tongue. When he spoke again it was in a gentler tone. It was almost as though it were he who was pleading.

'Don't you see how it is, honey? Don't you see what you're asking? You're telling me to throw away all I've worked for. Everything. My whole life.' He moved to her and began to stroke her hair, her neck. 'You do see, don't you? You see why I can't do it?'

'Yes,' she said, 'I see.'

She could have told him that there was no need to throw it all away; it had already gone. But she did not tell him that. She only wished he could accept the fact for himself.

'We'll manage,' he said. 'We'll manage, honey.'

\*   \*   \*

Moira Lycett was alone in the cabin when she heard the knock on the door. She was writing in her diary. She was one of those people who are habitual compilers of diaries; but she never kept them for long. As soon as a volume was full she threw it away; she had no desire to read any of it again and she was far too realistic to believe that what she had written would ever be of any value. In a way she supposed she wrote for therapeutic reasons, to get things out of her system. If she had had a bosom friend she might have confided in her; but she had never had a friend of that sort, not at least since her school-days, so instead she gave her confidences to the diary, which at any rate had the virtue of being thoroughly discreet.

The knock on the door sounded discreet too; just loud enough to be heard, not loud enough to be aggressive. She supposed it was the steward, and she called to him to come in without troubling to glance up from her writing.

She heard the door open and close. A voice that was certainly not the steward's said, 'Hope I'm not disturbing you, Mrs. Lycett.'

She looked up and saw that it was Perkins, the engineer, the man who had seen her wearing that ridiculous polythene cap after the fiasco of the bathroom. It was the memory of that encounter that caused her to colour slightly with anger when she saw who the visitor was.

'What do you want?'

Perkins smiled. It was probable that he too was remembering the earlier encounter, remembering it perhaps with more relish than Moira Lycett was.

'I've come about the fan.'

She saw then that he was carrying a tool-box in his hand. With the other he rubbed his cheek, as though massaging it, gazing all the while at the woman with his bright, beady eyes that put her in mind of some small species of rodent, a rat perhaps.

'It's not working, I hear.'

'I suppose my husband told you.'

'Not directly. The message was passed on, as you might say. I'm the electrician in this ship.'

'Then you'd better get on with the job. It's stifling in here.'

'It's all a question of what you get used to. It's worse in my cabin. Nearer the engine-room, see.'

'I'm not interested in your cabin.'

'No? Pity. If you were, I'd be only too pleased to show you round. No etchings, mind; but you can't have everything, can you?'

'I think you'd better get on with what you came for and then leave,' Moira Lycett said tartly.

She turned her back on him and began to write again in her diary. The insinuation in his words angered her. She would have got up and left the cabin, but that would have been a kind of triumph for him which she refused to concede. She heard him chuckle softly as he opened the tool-box. After that there were other sounds as he operated on the fan. She felt certain that he kept glancing at her as he worked, but she did not turn her head. Nevertheless, the mere fact of his presence made it impossible for her to write coherently; her pen moved, but what appeared on the paper was little better than gibberish, and this made her only the more angry with the engineer and with herself.

After a time she heard him say, 'Well now, that should have fixed it.'

Then there was the click of a switch and the sound of the fan whirring, and she could feel the air blowing on the back of her neck.

'Is that better, Mrs. Lycett?'

'Yes,' she said. 'Thank you, Mr. Perkins.' But still she did not turn. She waited to hear the sound of the door as he left the cabin.

But she heard no such sound. Instead, she felt something warm touch her neck where it curved towards the shoulder, something warm and soft and slightly moist.

She was so amazed at his audacity that she did not even move. He must have taken this lack of reaction for acquiescence, for she felt his hands exploring and heard his voice whispering in her ear. She was nauseated by the odour of bad breath and stale sweat that came from him, and she tried to slip away sideways off the chair. But his arms were round her, his hands cupping her breasts, and he was stronger than she would have imagined.

She could feel his mouth on her cheek now, moving down along the curve of her chin to her throat. She raised her feet and pressed them against the bulkhead under the hinged table, then straightened the legs abruptly, thrusting hard back on the chair. The sudden move took Perkins by surprise; the wooden back of the chair dug into his stomach and caused him to loose his grip. Moira Lycett took advantage of this loosening to wrench herself free. She turned to face him, flushed and raging.

'You filthy little swine!'

She lashed out with her hand, striking him on the left cheek with her open palm. He moved hastily back out of range, crestfallen. He put his fingers to his cheek where her sharp nails had drawn blood.

'Now, Mrs. Lycett, there was no call for that. You don't have to put on the outraged wife act, not for me. We both know you like having a man around.'

'A man! You flatter yourself.'

An angry glitter came into his eyes and a sneer into his voice. 'Maybe you like them a size bigger. Bigger and boneheaded. Is that the trouble?'

'Get out.' Her voice was low, trembling slightly with suppressed fury.

He took his fingers away from his cheek and looked at the blood on them with an evil lopsided grin. 'You've got sharp claws. Maybe I'd better give somebody who'll remain nameless a friendly warning. Tell him to watch out for himself because the cat can scratch.'

'Will you go?' she said. 'Or must I call for assistance and have you ejected?'

'Oh, I'll go.' He picked up his tool-box. 'I've done what I came for.' He opened the door, then turned and again gave the lopsided grin. 'I like to give satisfaction, Mrs. Lycett.' He went out of the cabin and closed the door softly behind him.

Moira Lycett gripped the side of the upper bunk with both hands and let the stream of air from the fan blow on her face. She felt dirty, soiled by Perkins's touch and by his insinuations. Did she look so easy that even a creature like that might try his luck?

The current of air gradually cooled her, gently stirring her chestnut hair, fanning her heated cheeks and brow. Perkins's words repeated themselves in her mind: 'Maybe you like them a size bigger.' So others had taken note of her conversations with Carl Johansen. On board ship there were always eyes watching, tongues wagging. Well, let them wag. Perhaps she would really give them something to wag about. If she already had the reputation, why not have the pleasure also?

She looked down and saw the cockroach

that Lycett had crushed, still sticking to the woodwork. With a shudder of disgust she turned away from the bunks, moved to the basin and began to wash. She had to wash away the imprint of Perkins's mouth, the contamination from her skin.

★ ★ ★

Mr. Finch was half-way through the first watch and not at all happy. It was not his duty that was worrying him — not at this particular time; it was a pleasant evening, acceptably cool after the heat of the day, there was no wind to speak of, and the Indian Ocean was as smooth as any ocean could ever be. One of the small dark seamen was at the wheel and Finch had just checked that he was keeping the *Chetwynd* on her correct course. The latest weather report that Maggs had brought gave no indication of any change for the worse and it looked as though the ship would have an uneventful run to Fremantle.

And yet Finch was very far from happy.

He stepped out of the wheelhouse on to the starboard wing of the bridge and looked at the sky. No clouds dimmed the brilliance of the stars shining in the infinite blackness of space; ahead the Southern Cross sparkled brightly, pointing the way the ship must go, and all around those other astral aids to navigation glittered like precious stones embedded in a vast slab of pitch.

Mr. Finch let his gaze fall to the bows of the ship, and he could detect the sudden surge of phosphorescence as the iron ploughshare thrust aside a myriad tiny living things that had the salt water for their home; creatures from which this strange luminosity emanated that seemed like liquid fire flowing past to port and starboard until it was quenched and lost in the fading wake of the ship.

Mr. Finch saw no beauty in any of these natural phenomena. He was interested in the stars only insofar as they had to be studied for the purposes of navigation, and though he had, times without number, seen the phosphorescence in the water, he had never once bothered to inquire what was the cause of it. On this night especially he was too deep in his own thoughts, his own worries, to be much concerned with anything else.

For the plain fact of the matter was that Mr. Finch was in love.

And of course it was Maggs whom he had to thank. If Maggs had not suggested going to that house he would never have seen the girl and it would never have happened. He still could not understand why on earth he had gone ashore with Maggs; after all, he didn't even like the fellow. It just happened that they had got to the head of the gangway at the same time, and as they were both obviously going ashore alone he felt almost compelled to invite Maggs to have a drink with him.

Maggs himself seemed not at all keen on the idea; Finch had noticed before how unsociable the radio officer was; but after thinking it over for a moment or two he accepted the invitation.

So they went to a bar and the drink expanded into two and then into three, and finally more than he could remember. It was well on into the evening by then and suddenly Maggs, quite out of the blue, said he knew a house where they could have some congenial female company and why not go there?

'You mean girls?' Finch said. His mind was not working quite as quickly as usual and things took a little time to get through. 'Girls?'

Maggs nodded his head wisely. 'What else would I be meaning?'

Finch also nodded. 'Could be the very thing to complete the pleasure of the evening.' And he had to speak the words very carefully because they had a way of becoming slurred.

Maggs stood up. 'Okay then. Let's go.'
'Let's go,' Finch said.

★  ★  ★

Her name was Ah Mai or something of the kind. She spoke a funny kind of twittering English and Finch could understand only half what she said. But what did that matter? She looked wonderful with those mysterious black, slanting eyes and that mysterious, half-shy, half-inviting smile which made Finch's heart beat faster whenever she turned it on him. She was wearing a long Chinese dress of green silk, tightly fitting, high at the throat, and with a slit in one side that revealed her leg up to the thigh. It was the kind of leg that was worth revealing.

Finch thought she was far better than the girl Maggs had got. Maggs's girl was shorter and dumpier, and she had a wider, coarser face. She was not really in the same league as Ah Mai. But Maggs seemed satisfied.

'You've been here before then?' Finch said. He had been in the same ship with Maggs for a couple of years and he realised now that he still knew nothing whatever about him.

'A few times,' Maggs admitted.

They had more drinks. There was music

coming from somewhere, a kind of juke-box with oriental overtones. A few couples were dancing — if you could call it dancing; they hardly moved, just seemed glued to one another, swaying a little. The room had embroidered hangings, alcoves here and there, a lot of bamboo; and there was an indefinable odour which Finch, for no reason at all, immediately associated with the smoking of opium. He had never smelt an opium pipe, but that was what he was sure it would have smelt like if he had.

He was now more than a little drunk and he kept pulling out his wallet and giving out paper money as though he were dealing a hand of cards. Maggs for his part seemed to be quite unaffected by the alcohol he had consumed; now and then Finch noticed the radio officer looking at him with an expression that might have been described as one of malicious amusement, not unmixed with contempt. Even with the haze of intoxication clouding his susceptibilities, he still knew that he really did not like Maggs and that Maggs most certainly did not like him. The fact that they were out on the town together did not mean that they had suddenly become bosom chums; it was a purely fortuitous excursion that would probably never be repeated.

'Enjoy yourself,' Maggs said. 'Throw away all restraint. Let your bloody self go.'

★ ★ ★

Ah Mai's room was up a flight of stairs and along a corridor so dimly lighted that it was like going into a cave. Ah Mai went on ahead and Finch caught exciting glimpses of her thigh breaking through the slit in the green silk dress. She came to the room, opened the door, switched the light on, smiled at Finch.

'You come in?'

Finch went in and Ah Mai closed the door. The room was not really big enough for the bed; it left very little space for the other furniture, even less for people. The girl stripped quickly with sinuous, wriggling movements. Finch thought of a snake casting its skin, but there was really nothing snakelike about Ah Mai.

She had a lovely soft, resilient body, golden yellow skin as smooth as satin and small, firm breasts with impudent little nipples. She seemed to have one thought only — to give him pleasure. Lying with her on the big bed, Finch gave himself up to sensual delight. He would have liked to stay there for ever, caught in this honeyed dream of infinite sweetness, never to return to the ship, to Captain

Leach's biting tongue, to all the worries, the responsibilities of his hated job. He kissed her mouth, her throat, her breasts. Her limbs twined themselves about him; her tongue made playful, darting explorations; they scarcely spoke a word. Oh God, dear God, he thought, let this last for ever and ever, Amen.

But it could not last for ever. He had to get back to the ship, to the cold, sober realities of life, to his own incompetencies as a sailor, to the searing criticisms of Captain Leach and the brutal scorn of Mr. Johansen. He had to go back from heaven into hell.

Nevertheless, Finch had returned to the house another night — without Maggs; he had gone back to Ah Mai. And after that he had gone to her many more times while the *Chetwynd* remained loading in Hong Kong; and there could be no doubt about it — he had fallen deeply, irrevocably in love with this utterly enchanting Chinese girl.

He talked with Ah Mai on these later visits and he believed that she loved him too — unless she was simply playing a game with him. That was what plagued his mind now that so many hundreds of miles of sea divided them — the thought, indeed the fear, that she had just been playing with him; that and the knowledge that while he was away there would be other men with her, other men enjoying her. When he thought about those other men with Ah Mai Finch's mind squirmed with agony; it was mental torture. And every day and every night he tortured himself again and again with pictures of Ah Mai, his darling Ah Mai, in the brutal arms of other men.

★ ★ ★

Finch did not hear Maggs approach. The radio officer wore rubber-soled shoes and had a habit of creeping silently about, as though intent on taking people by surprise. Finch gave an involuntary start when he became aware of the other man's presence, and this was not lost on Maggs.

'Well now, Third,' he said. 'Keeping a sharp lookout like you're supposed to do? Not dozing off in the balmy night air, eh?'

'What do you want?' Finch demanded, his voice edgy.

'Nothing. Do I have to want anything? Can't I just come to pass the time of day — or night?'

'I didn't know you were so sociable.'

'Don't you like my company?'

Finch did not answer. He rested his elbows on the bleached teak rail in front of him and stared ahead. He could feel the muted throbbing of the ship's engines coming up through the superstructure, and now and then he caught the acrid tang of fumes drifting from the funnel. He did not want Maggs's company. He wished the fellow would go away and leave him to his dreams of Ah Mai.

'Nice weather,' Maggs said; and he gave a low chuckle, as though the very idea amused him. 'Maybe it'll stay that way. Maybe.'

'Is there any reason why it shouldn't?' Finch asked.

'Reason? No; no reason. No reason at all.'

He began to walk away.

'Sparks,' Finch called.

Maggs stopped, came back. 'Well?'

Finch looked at him, looked away, drummed on the rail with his fingers.

'Out with it,' Maggs said. 'If you've got something to say, say it.' He sounded impatient.

'That girl,' Finch said.

'What girl?'

'In Hong Kong. Ah Mai.'

'Oh, her. What about her?'

Finch hesitated. Should he confide in Maggs? He hesitated, decided not to after all. 'Nothing.'

Maggs drew closer, stared up into Finch's face in the dim light. 'Hey now; don't tell me you've gone and fallen for that little whore. No, that would be too rich. Not that little yellow whore.'

Finch rounded on him in sudden fury. 'Don't call her that.'

'Whore? Why not? That's what she is, isn't it?'

Finch could not deny the fact; which made it all the worse to hear Maggs bringing out the word with that kind of gloating relish.

'Well, well, well,' Maggs said. 'Just one night and she's got you hooked.'

'It wasn't just one night.'

'No?' Maggs sounded surprised. 'So you went there again? Without telling me. You sly devil.'

'Why should I tell you?'

'No reason, I suppose. Still, I did introduce you. So now you're in love. Well, you'll be able to see her again when we get back to Hong Kong. She'll be there waiting for you at the end of each trip. That end anyway.'

'I want to get her out of that place,' Finch said.

Maggs stared at him. 'Have you gone out of your mind? Even if there were no other obstacles, what makes you think she'd come?'

'I think she would. I think she loves me.'

Maggs gave a derisive laugh. 'The trouble with you, Finch boy, is you've got a romantic soul. Maybe you've been reading too many love stories.' He put his hand on Finch's sleeve. 'What do you think she's up to while you're away? This very minute maybe.'

Finch was silent. He could imagine only too vividly. It was that which was torturing him. And perhaps Maggs guessed as much and took a sadistic delight in turning the knife in the wound.

'I'll give you three guesses,' Maggs said, and sniggered. 'Though really you shouldn't need more than one.'

Finch shook the hand off his sleeve. 'Go away.' His voice rose to a squeak. 'Go away and leave me alone. I've got things to do.'

'You've got things to do all right,' Maggs said. But he went away. Finch could hear him humming a tune as he went. The revelation of the third mate's unfortunate love affair seemed to have cheered him.

'Damn him!' Finch muttered. 'Damn him to hell!' He regretted confiding in Maggs. It had been madness to do so. It had done no good. All it had done was to give Maggs a laugh. And now perhaps he would broadcast the story all round the ship, so that everybody could have a laugh. Damn him! Damn him!

But in fact Finch need have had no fear that Maggs would tell anyone else. Maggs was quite content to keep the information locked up securely in his own mind. He had no desire to share it with anyone.

Finch was still turning over in his mind ways and means of getting Ah Mai away from the house in Hong Kong when he handed over the watch at midnight to Mr. Prior, the second mate.

Edward Prior was nearly sixty and the chief reason why he had never risen any higher in the Merchant Service was that he had never had any desire to do so. He was reasonably competent, but he was too easy-going, inclined to be slovenly in his dress, and utterly lacking in ambition. He was a bachelor, about medium height, rather plump, slightly stiff in the left leg, grey-haired and rosy-cheeked, and equipped with such a badly fitting set of false teeth that they made a clicking noise like castanets whenever he happened to be eating. Captain Leach once remarked sourly that all they needed was a guitar and they might have some Spanish dancing. Far from being offended, Mr. Prior laughed more than anyone, which was rather unwise, because when he laughed the upper set was always in danger of dropping out.

Mr. Prior was such a fatherly sort of man that Finch had half a mind to confide in him and ask his advice. In fact he lingered on the bridge for a time, watching Prior fill and light an old, bitten-down pipe. Prior noticed with no little surprise this unusual reluctance of the third mate to cut away to his bunk.

'Something on your mind, lad?'

Finch gave a little cough, almost came out with it, then decided not to. After all, what good would it do? He had told Maggs and no good had come of that, only derision.

'No,' he said. 'Nothing. Nothing at all. Good night.'

He turned and walked away. Ned Prior sucked thoughtfully at his pipe and watched him go.

# 5

## China Tea

'I shall have to go,' Moira Lycett said.

Carl Johansen stretched out a bare, muscular arm and restrained her. With that arm lying across her body she could not get up; it held her like an iron band. But an iron band would never have been so warm, so vitally alive; would not have sent those ripples of pleasure going through her.

'No hurry.'

'It's getting late. Morton will have finished his game.'

'We have not finished our game.' He pressed his mouth against her throat where the pulse throbbed.

'If he goes back to the cabin and I'm not there he'll wonder where I am.'

'That bothers you?'

'I don't like arguments.'

'Arguments! Hell with arguments!'

'That's all very well for you.'

'Sure is all very well for me. Is fine.'

'But it's late.'

'Not so late. I am off duty till morning watch.'

'Morning watch?'

'Four to eight.'

'You'll want some sleep.'

'Hell with sleep. People die in sleep.'

The mate's cabin was slightly bigger than those allotted to the passengers, though it had only one bunk. Moira Lycett had not made up her mind until the last moment whether or not to go to him. Johansen had been waiting, confident that she would come. Too confident, she thought. It galled her a little, this obvious belief of his that he was irresistible, that he had only to beckon and she must come running. She did not like anyone to take her for granted.

Morton was playing cards with the Australian, Grade. She felt sure no one had seen her enter Johansen's cabin, but if Morton finished his game and found that she was missing he might have suspicions. She was not in the habit of walking on deck at that hour.

'I must go.'

He took his arm away. 'Okay. Is always tomorrow.'

She slid away from him and stood up. 'I don't know.'

Johansen reached out a long arm and

hooked her round the waist, pulling her against the bunk. She felt his wide, hard mouth pressing into her side just above the hip.

'Sure you know. Tomorrow you come. Same time.'

Again his mouth pressed her side. She felt a strange weakness in all her limbs, as though the bones had turned to water. Johansen looked magnificent in his nakedness; a big, strong, virile animal.

'Let me go,' she whispered. It was like a prayer. 'Let me go, Carl.'

He released her suddenly and she almost fell. She had to clutch at the bunk to steady herself. Johansen laughed softly.

'You got no strength in the legs? The so lovely, lovely legs. Is so?'

'You let go of me so suddenly. I wasn't prepared.'

'So? You want I should hold you again?' There was a hint of mockery in his voice. In his eyes too.

She felt suddenly angry — with him, with herself. She guessed that he thought her cheap, easy to get. He would probably boast about his conquest later. Damn him then. But she knew that tomorrow she would come to him again.

He lay in the bunk and watched her while

she dressed. 'I think I sleep good now,' he said. 'I think I have pleasant dreams.'

'You won't sleep long. Not if you have to be on watch at four.'

'I don't need much sleep. You work in ships, that's the way it's got to be. Sleep when you can. Bits and pieces.'

When she was ready to go she unlocked the door and opened it cautiously. She could see no one outside. She slipped out of the cabin and closed the door quickly behind her. The alleyway smelt of hot oil and fresh paint, a close, heavy atmosphere that oppressed her. She descended an internal stairway to a lower deck and walked down another alleyway to her own cabin.

She believed she had not been observed leaving Johansen's quarters, but she was mistaken. One person had seen her leave; one person who had been on the lookout and had made certain that he himself should not be seen. When Moira Lycett had gone that person also went away.

Morton Lycett was in the cabin when Moira went in. He did not look pleased.

★ ★ ★

'Where the devil have you been? It's nearly midnight.'

117

She closed the door before answering. She searched for a cigarette and lit it. She was annoyed to notice that her hand shook slightly.

'I asked a question.' Lycett sounded edgy. 'Where have you been?'

She let the smoke flow from her mouth with a sigh. 'I don't see that it's any concern of yours, but if you're really so interested, I've been on deck.'

'At this hour?'

'It's a pleasant night.'

'You've been up there a hell of a time. I've been in here since half-past ten.'

'You finished your game early.'

He gave her a quick, suspicious glance. 'You expected it to last longer?'

She answered offhandedly, as though it were a matter of no importance, 'It usually does.'

'So you time me?'

'Don't be an idiot, Morton.'

'Perhaps I'm not such an idiot as you take me for. Was anyone with you on deck?'

'No. I was alone.'

'I should have thought you'd find it chilly, dressed like that.'

'It makes a pleasant change to be cool.'

He was silent for a time, but he was watching her. It was something he had started doing lately, just watching her. The knowledge that his eyes were on her even when she turned her back on him irritated her. She preferred his complaints to that silent scrutiny; it got on her nerves.

At last he said, 'You couldn't have been on deck all that time. I went up and looked for you.'

'You didn't look closely enough.'

'This isn't the *Queen Elizabeth*. There's not all that deck area. If you'd been there I'd have found you.'

She affected boredom. 'I don't know where this interrogation is supposed to be leading. Again, if you're interested, I wasn't on deck all the time.'

'Where were you?'

'With the Mensteins.'

She realised at once that she had made a blunder. Morton would quite possibly check up. Perhaps she had better speak to the Mensteins first thing in the morning. But could she really ask them to provide an alibi? It would be too degrading. And suppose they refused to play? She had scarcely spoken to them beyond the ordinary courtesies, but she had gained the impression that they were the kind of people who would probably have a respect for the truth. No, better not to say anything to them. If Morton discovered that she had lied, so be it. She could always laugh it off.

But could she? It was becoming rather less easy to turn away Morton's questions with a laugh. Ridiculous as it might seem, he appeared to be becoming more possessive as he grew older. Surely he could not still be in love with her after all these years. Or was it not so much love as a sense of property? No doubt he considered that she belonged to him and perhaps he resented the idea that any other man should lay a hand on something that was legally his. Perhaps even Morton could be as old-fashioned as that.

She glanced at him. He was half-sitting, half-lying on his bunk and frowning. He seemed to be in a really black mood; perhaps he had lost money to the Australian at cards. So what if he found out about her and Johansen? He already suspected; that was obvious. But suppose suspicion hardened into certainty? What would he do then? She simply did not know. Morton might not be a courageous man but he could be very vindictive; that she knew. Well, she would just have to be careful; make sure no one saw her entering or leaving the mate's cabin. Then Morton might suspect all he liked, but he would have no proof and she could meet any accusation with a denial.

Nevertheless, it was a pity she had brought in the Mensteins.

'There's something I want you to remember,' Lycett said.

'And what would that be?'

'That you're still my wife.'

'God,' she said, 'do you think I'm ever likely to forget it?'

★   ★   ★

'What's in the box, Nick?' Grade asked.

Holt held the box in his two hands. He had taken it out of the wardrobe to get at a book on the same shelf. The box measured about ten inches by six and was perhaps five inches deep. It was made of plywood, roughly nailed together, and there were some Chinese characters painted on it.

'Just tea. China tea.'

'You like China tea?'

'I don't,' Holt said. 'Mr. Saunders asked me to take it to his partner in Perth. Seems he's crazy about the stuff.'

Saunders was the Australian wool merchant who had paid Holt's passage from Hong Kong and had offered him a job. The partner's name was Roylance. Saunders had not given Holt Roylance's address but he had said that he would send the man a cable and tell him to meet Holt off the ship in Fremantle. Holt thought this was very kind of Mr. Saunders, and said so.

'Think nothing of it,' Saunders said. 'I think I'm getting a good man. I'm sure of it.'

'But it's not really necessary for Mr. Roylance to come to Fremantle. I can find my own way to Perth.'

'You ever been to Perth?'

Holt admitted that he had not.

'Then let Fred Roylance be your guide.'

'Perhaps he won't want to be put to all that bother.'

'For him a trip to Fremantle is no bother at all. I'll tell him about the tea and he'll come like a bat out of hell. Give old Fred the scent of China tea and he'll go anywhere. Me, I can't stand the muck. Especially this blend; it's Lapsang Souchong. Tastes like tar.'

Holt wondered why anyone should like drinking tar, but every man to his taste. All he had to do was take the box to Fremantle and hand it over to Roylance. That should be easy enough.

'How'd you happen to bump into this man Saunders?' Grade asked.

'Just chance. I was having a drink in a bar. He accidentally jogged my elbow and spilt my beer. Of course he apologised, bought me another, and we got talking. He's an easy man to talk to.'

'So you told him you were down to your last cent, and he offered you a job and the passage money. Just like that?'

'More or less.'

Grade patted Holt on the shoulder. 'Congratulations, chum. I don't know what you've got, but it must be something. Nobody ever made up to me like that just for spilling my drink. Maybe it's that Pommy charm.'

'Maybe it is.'

'And all you have to do in return is take that little old box to the man in Fremantle. My, my.'

There was something in Grade's tone that Holt did not altogether care for. Grade sounded cynical. His expression was cynical too.

'Don't you believe me?'

'Oh, I believe you, chum,' Grade said. 'It's Mr. Saunders I find just a wee bit hard to believe. All that milk of human kindness oozing out of every pore.'

'I don't get you.'

'You ever read a book called 'Nicholas Nickleby'? Written by a character name of Charles Dickens.'

'I know who wrote 'Nicholas Nickleby'. I read it a long time ago.'

'Remember the Cheeryble Brothers?'

'Vaguely.'

'The Cheerybles gave our Nicholas a job just because they liked the look of him.'

'So?'

Grade smiled, and it was a very cynical smile. 'Me, I never did believe people like the Cheerybles existed in real life. Not today. Though there are certainly some Nicholases drifting around.'

'What are you trying to say?' Holt asked.

'What I'm trying to say is this: if I were you, Nick, I'd open that box and take a good hard look at that China tea. Yes, sir, I'd open it right here and now.'

'You're crazy. Why should I do that?'

'Well, let's just say in the interests of research. The widening of knowledge. You ever seen any Lapsang Souchong tea?'

'No, but — '

'Nor me either. I'd like to though. Yes, I truly would like to see a handful of that stuff.'

'And how do I explain to Mr. Roylance why his box is bust open?'

'You don't have to explain anything. You can nail it up again.'

Holt gave Grade a long silent stare. Grade stared back, still with the cynical smile on his face.

Then Holt said, 'Have you got a lever?'

Grade produced a clasp-knife with a

screwdriver attachment. 'I was in the Boy Scouts. They taught me to be prepared.'

Holt put the plywood box on the table. He took Grade's knife and inserted the screwdriver under the lid. The lid was held down by thin half-inch nails; a little leverage with the screwdriver prised it up, drawing the nails out of the wood with a slight creaking sound. Holt put the lid carefully on one side. There was some tinfoil covering the contents. He folded the tinfoil back and revealed nothing but tea.

He looked at Grade. 'Satisfied?'

Grade was still smiling. 'So that's Lapsang Souchong.'

Holt bent down and sniffed the tea. Saunders had been dead right about the flavour; it even smelt of tar.

'How about a brew-up?' Grade said.

Holt began to fold back the tinfoil. He had had just about enough of Grade's little jokes. He had been a fool to open the box. Now what was he going to use for a hammer to knock the lid back on?

'Wait a second,' Grade said. He stepped to the table and poked a finger in the tea. Then he picked up the box and emptied the contents out on to the table.

'Here,' Holt protested. 'What the devil do you think you're up to?'

'You've been short-weighted, chum.'

'Short-weighted?'

'You've only got half a box of tea.'

Holt peered into the box. It looked strangely shallow.

'False bottom,' Grade said. 'Why?'

'You tell me.'

'Maybe I will when we've looked deeper.'

Grade picked up the knife, opened the large blade and forced it between the false bottom and the side of the box; after a little manipulation a rectangle of thin plywood came out. Beneath it, rammed in so that it completely filled the available space, was a polythene bag containing what appeared to be a white, crystalline powder.

Grade made a soft hissing sound through his teeth. 'Now that, Nick, boy, doesn't look like any tea I ever saw. You know something? I begin to think your Mr. Saunders wasn't being altogether honest with you. Not strictly on the up and up, if you get my meaning. Fact is, I think you got a crook deal.'

He lifted the bag out of the box. It was fastened with a piece of fine string. Grade untied the string and opened the bag. He took a little of the powder on his finger and touched it with the tip of his tongue.

'Bitter taste. What does that tell you, Nick?'

'Nothing.'

'It tells me something. It tells me this is heroin for a cert.'

'Heroin! Are you sure?'

'I'd lay a thousand to one.'

'It can't be,' Holt said; but he was thinking it very well could be just that. And he did not like it.

'Just look at it this way,' Grade said. 'This comes from Hong Kong. Red China is just across the border. In China the poppies grow that opium is extracted from. Morphine comes from opium. Heroin is a derivative of morphine. Are you with me?'

'I'm with you,' Holt said, and wished he wasn't.

Grade weighed the bag in his hand. 'You any idea what this little lot would be worth on the black market?'

Holt shook his head.

Grade appeared to be making a mental calculation. Then he said, 'I'm guessing, mind, but if this is heroin — and somehow I can't see Mr. Saunders bothering to hide a bag of salt away like that; if it is heroin I'd say at a low estimate it'd be worth not less than somewhere around forty thousand Australian dollars. Say twenty thousand pounds sterling.'

'You must be joking. Twenty thousand pounds for that.'

'You can get anything between one and four pounds a grain, so they tell me.'

Holt wondered just who 'they' were, but he did not ask.

'So that's why Mr. Roylance was going to be so willing to meet me in Fremantle. Nothing to do with China tea.'

'Oh, he may have a taste for that too.' Grade re-tied the bag with the thin string. 'Seems to me, Nick, you were the stooge. If the customs found that junk you were the one who got caught. Not Mr. Saunders, who is probably not really Mr. Saunders anyway, and not Mr. Roylance, who is likewise probably not Mr. Roylance; just you, chum, just you.'

'Joe Soap.'

'You said it. But the chances were good that you'd get through without even having the box opened. You got that innocent look. It was a good play. How was Saunders to know that you'd have such a suspicious bastard for a cabin mate? I wonder how many innocent suckers he uses like this.'

'So much for the job in Australia,' Holt said. He could see now that there never would have been a job. He was just being used; and when he had served his purpose he would have been discarded. He no longer believed there had been any accident about that spilt beer; it had all been planned.

'Cheer up,' Grade said. 'Plenty other jobs. What are you going to do about this?' He indicated the bag of heroin.

Holt picked up the bag and put it back in the box. He pushed the false bottom into place and began to scoop up the tea and refill the box.

'I'm going to hand it over to the customs when we reach port.'

'They'll ask questions.'

'I'll answer them. I haven't got anything to hide.'

He folded the tinfoil over the tea, picked up a shoe and began to hammer the lid on with the heel. When he had finished the box looked almost exactly as it had when Saunders had given it to him.

Grade was looking thoughtful. 'You could still get that through customs with no questions asked.'

'Are you suggesting I should play Saunders' game for him? Take the box to Roylance.'

'Who said anything about taking it to Roylance?'

Holt stared at Grade. 'Now what exactly do you mean by that?'

'For a share of the takings,' Grade said coolly, 'I could introduce you to a customer for that stuff. A fifty-fifty share. Of course we'd have to go to Sydney; that's where the market is. We could get a better price in London or New York maybe, but we might have trouble getting the merchandise there. Sydney's the best bet.'

Holt wondered whether the Australian was joking, but when he looked into Grade's eyes he knew there was no joke about it. So what sort of a man was this, who knew people who were in the market for smuggled drugs?

'You must be mad. Do you think I'm a crook?'

Grade lit a cigarette. There was a steely glint in his eyes. 'I never knew the man who wasn't crook enough to pick up ten thousand pounds lying at his feet.'

Holt put the box back in his wardrobe and closed the door. He was sweating. He didn't want to listen to Grade. He wanted to get out of the cabin, get away from Grade, anywhere. But he stayed where he was. Grade's voice had a harsh, slightly nasal intonation, and yet it was as seductive as the Sirens' song. He stayed and listened.

'Ten thousand pounds sterling,' Grade said. 'All that clear profit. No income tax.'

★ ★ ★

Victor Maggs sat in the wireless cabin and listened to the weather report. There was a smile on Maggs's face as he heard the storm warning. He had heard quite a lot about Jessie since that first report, and by Maggs's reckoning there was now little doubt that Jessie and the *Chetwynd* would in the not too distant future come to grips.

As he listened to the flat, metallic voice coming through the headphones Maggs experienced a fluttering sensation in his stomach. Tremors of excitement rippled through his body, not unmingled with dread. But even in the dread he took a certain masochistic pleasure, and however much afraid he might be, the fear was more than counter-balanced by the thought of revenging himself on Captain Leach.

And not only on Leach but on all the rest of them; on that Major Lycett with his damned public school accent which grated on Maggs's ear; on that snooty Mrs. Lycett who only had time for the mate; on the mate too; yes, especially on the mate, whom Maggs hated for his handsome face, his physical perfection, his self-assurance, even for his nationality.

Maggs chuckled softly. They didn't know what was coming to them. Only he knew; only he could avert the disaster; and he did not wish to do so. He felt like a god, controlling the fate of so many people. The chuckle became louder; it grew to laughter; the laughter shook Maggs's stunted body; it was wild, insane. He laughed until the tears rolled down his cheeks. A god! He, a god!

# 6

## Truth

Mr. Johansen attacked his breakfast with zest. There was nothing, he always maintained, like the morning watch to give a man an appetite for the first meal of the day. And the mate was not fussy about what he ate: curry and rice, bacon and eggs, toast and marmalade, it all disappeared into his voracious mouth. However little sleep he might have had during the night, he did not look tired. He had not shaved and there was golden bristle on his chin, but his eyes were clear and wide awake.

Lycett watched him covertly with distaste. Lycett had very little appetite; he merely pecked gloomily at his food, as though he suspected that the Chinese cook might have slipped some deadly poison into it.

Moira Lycett was not present; she seldom appeared for breakfast, preferring to sleep on until a later hour. Captain Leach was not in the dining saloon either, but his reasons for absence were different. Leach's breakfast took the form of whisky and he consumed it in the privacy of his own quarters. The Mensteins and the Easts were there, Nick Holt and Tom Grade, Mr. Prior, the engineers at their separate table, and Radio Officer Maggs. Mr. Finch, whose watch it was, was on the bridge.

Two large overhead fans revolved at no great speed and with a slight, monotonous creaking sound, as though after so many years of service their joints had developed arthritis. The portholes along one side had been open all night and the air, stirred by the fans, was a little fresher than it would become later in the day. Conversation was desultory, with long pauses when nobody seemed to have anything to say and the only sounds were the rattle of the cutlery and china, the creaking of the fans and the clicking of Mr. Prior's teeth.

Perkins ate with his head close to his plate, as though he had made a time and motion study and had decided that this saved a lot of work for the arms. From this bowed position he shot secret glances across at the mate on the other table and then at Lycett; and now and then, in the intervals between chewing, the shadow of a smile twisted his thin lips.

Johansen chanced to notice the smile. He said, 'You find something funny, Mr. Perkins? You grin so much.'

Perkins raised his head and his beady eyes regarded the mate for a moment or two, the smile still hovering about his lips. 'Thoughts, Mr. Johansen. Just thoughts.'

'Mighty funny thoughts, mebbe. You tell us what these so funny thoughts are. Give us all a laugh.'

'I don't think you'd find them quite so amusing. In fact I think you wouldn't laugh at all if I told you.'

'No? So you don't tell us, how we know? Not right to keep good things to yourself.'

Perkins drank some coffee, put the cup down. 'Other people keep these good things to themselves.'

Lycett was looking at Perkins. There was something behind the little engineer's words, some hidden meaning; he was sure of it. Perkins had a secret, and Lycett, with sudden intuition, had the idea that that secret might be of concern to him as well as the mate. He noticed that there were some scratches on the engineer's cheek and he wondered how they had got there.

Johansen perhaps also had some inkling of what was in Perkins's mind, for he broke off the exchanges abruptly and turned his attention to Pearl East.

'I see you practising on deck. You keep your hand in.'

'We have to keep in practice, Mr. Johansen.'

'Is good act. I see plenty acts; I know what I talk about. Is mighty fine act. Sure.'

'I'm glad you think so.'

Sydney East ate in silence. He did not care for the way Johansen looked at his wife; it was something he had noticed before; when Johansen talked to her his eyes seemed to be saying other things, things that made him, Syd East, burn inside. Why could Johansen not be content with turning his charm on one woman, on Mrs. Lycett? But there were men like that, men who would go for any attractive woman, no matter whose wife she might be. And there could be no doubt that Johansen had charm; you had to admit that, even if you hated the man's guts.

He glanced at his wife. She was looking at Johansen and smiling radiantly. So was even she attracted by this big, blond Dane? He dismissed the idea; Pearl was not like that, not like Mrs. Lycett; she was just being polite. Try as he might, however, he could not altogether quench the flame of jealousy that had spurted up inside him. She need not surely have smiled quite so much.

'Some day,' Johansen was saying, 'mebbe I see you on stage. I give you big hand-clap. Sure.'

Pearl gave her little musical laugh. 'I'll look forward to that.'

'I send bouquet to dressing-room.'

'Don't waste your money,' East said, and his voice was so hard, so bitter, that even the Mensteins, who had been talking quietly to each other, became suddenly silent and looked at him in surprise.

There was a brief, awkward pause before Johansen gave a laugh. 'Waste to give flowers to a lovely lady? How so?'

East took a piece of toast and broke it in his hands. 'Flowers die.'

'All things die,' Lycett said, and he was looking at Johansen.

Maggs gave a snigger. 'You're right, Major. Oh, how right you are.'

Conversation flagged. A blight seemed to have fallen on the breakfast table. The fans creaked on.

★ ★ ★

Maggs had just left the dining saloon when he felt a tap on the shoulder. He turned his head and saw Johansen towering over him. Maggs disliked being tapped on the shoulder; he disliked being forced to look up to people as tall as the mate.

'A word with you, Sparks,' Johansen said.

'A word! What word?'

Johansen grasped Maggs's arm and drew him away from the saloon, out of earshot of the passengers.

'What d'you want?' Maggs demanded. He liked the mate's grip on his arm even less than the tap on the shoulder. He even felt vaguely alarmed. Johansen was so big and strong. Nobody had a right to be so husky.

Johansen stopped propelling Maggs along the alleyway. Maggs had his back against a handrail and Johansen stood facing him.

Maggs felt surrounded.

'The glass is falling,' Johansen said.

Maggs felt a sense of relief, and was angry with himself for having been nervous enough to feel relieved. Had he imagined the mate was going to beat him up? What a ridiculous idea. And yet it had been in his head.

'So the glass is falling. What of it?'

'When glass fall, bad weather about. Fall a lot, mebbe bloody bad.'

'Has it fallen a lot?'

'Not yet. I think mebbe later.'

'Why tell me?'

'You are Sparks. You take weather reports.'

'So what?'

'All weather reports say weather set fine?'

'That's right.'

'No storms around? No bloody big winds?'

138

'Nothing.'

Johansen looked puzzled. 'Is strange. Me, I smell something. I feel something in my bones. Sure.'

'I wouldn't trust too much in bones,' Maggs said. 'I never heard of a met man forecasting from the feel of his bones.'

Johansen's face hardened. 'You laugh at me, huh?'

Maggs shook his head. 'Not me. I'm just saying I put more trust in the weather reports than in any man's feelings. The reports say no storms.'

But he was thinking: You bet I'm laughing at you, you great bonehead. I'm laughing at the whole flaming lot of you. Me, Victor Maggs, the little runt. I'm laughing.

'Strange,' Johansen said. 'Mighty strange. Mebbe my bones tell me wrong. Mebbe I get old.' He left Maggs and walked away shaking his head.

Maggs wanted to let out a hoot of derision at the mate's receding back, but he restrained the impulse. The time would come, and it would not be long now, not long at all. Mr. Johansen's bones were better prophets than even he suspected.

Lycett was about to open his cabin door and step inside when Perkins stopped him.

'I'd like to speak to you, Major.'

Lycett closed the half-opened door. 'On what subject?' He could think of nothing that Perkins could have to say that could possibly interest him.

'A subject of some importance.'

'Fire away then. I'm listening.'

'Not here, Major. Somewhere private. My cabin.'

'Your cabin? Now, look here, what the devil is this all about?'

'I'll tell you when we get there. Are you coming?'

'I'm damned if I see why I should.'

'I said it was important.' Perkins put a hand on Lycett's arm. Lycett looked down at it as he might have looked at some repulsive insect that had alighted on his sleeve. It was a scarred, knocked-about sort of hand with broken, blackened finger-nails. It was not difficult to divine that Perkins's work had to do with machinery; dirty machinery at that. 'Important to you, Major.'

Lycett was startled. He had begun to imagine that Perkins was going to ask him some kind of favour, but apparently it was nothing of the sort. He looked into Perkins's eyes and did not like what he saw. There was something evil there. Whatever Perkins wished to speak to him about, Lycett had a feeling that it was not going to be pleasant to listen to. He had half a mind to tell the fellow to go to the devil; but he did not.

'Very well,' he said. 'Lead the way.'

Perkins's cabin was small and rather squalid. It had an odour of stale cigarette smoke, stale sweat and oil. There was one chair. Perkins offered it to his guest. Lycett sat down only because it would have seemed ridiculous to have remained standing.

'Like a beer?' Perkins asked.

'No, thank you.'

'Cigarette?'

'No.' Lycett was becoming impatient. He believed Perkins was deliberately delaying, keeping him in suspense for sheer devilment. Damn the fellow!

Perkins lit a cigarette for himself and sat on the bunk. For a while he remained silent, just staring at Lycett.

'Well?' Lycett said testily. 'Let's have it. Something of importance, you said.'

'It's about your wife.'

Lycett's head jerked up. It was what he had been half expecting, for what else could Perkins have to talk to him about that would be of importance to him? And Perkins was the kind of sly, crafty devil who would be certain to ferret out something unsavoury if there was anything to ferret.

Lycett knew that he should have got up

and left the cabin then. It would have been the honourable thing to do, for an honourable man would have refused to hear anything about his wife from such a creature. But honour was a dead duck. Lycett wanted to know what Perkins had to say.

'What about my wife?'

Perkins watched the smoke drifting away from his cigarette. But he was watching Lycett too. 'I saw her last night.'

'That's not surprising. I imagine a lot of other people saw her too.'

'Not where I saw her.'

Lycett felt an almost irresistible desire to plant his fist in Perkins's mean little mouth. But he did not move.

'Oh,' he said.

'Do you want to know where it was?'

'You're going to tell me anyway. That was the object of bringing me here, I imagine.'

Perkins looked a little put out. 'Well, you don't have to take that tone, Major. I'm only trying to help you.'

'Help me, be damned!' Lycett said. 'You know as well as I do that you're only doing this for the pleasure it gives you to tell tales. And maybe because you want to get your own back on somebody. But go on.'

'I'm not so sure that I will go on now.' Perkins had an injured air. 'You try to do what's right and that's all the thanks you get.'

'Go on, damn you!'

'No, to hell with it,' Perkins said. 'I won't go on.'

Lycett got up from the chair, grabbed the front of Perkins's shirt in both hands and shook him. He even banged Perkins's head on the bulkhead behind the bunk. Perkins gave a howl. Lycett was really hurting him.

'All right. All right. I'll tell you.'

Lycett released him and sat down again, breathing heavily.

Perkins said sulkily, 'You didn't have to do that. There was no need for violence. I was going to tell you anyway, like you said. She was going into the mate's cabin.'

He had been expecting it, but it was like a stab in the heart all the same. But he kept his voice under control. 'What time was this?'

'About nine-fifteen.'

Lycett's eyes narrowed. It fitted. At nine-fifteen he had already been playing cards with Grade for a quarter of an hour. She had waited until he was safely out of the way. Damn her!

'You want to know what time she came out?' Perkins asked.

'At eleven forty-five,' Lycett said.

Perkins looked like a man who had just seen his ace trumped. 'You knew?'

'No, I didn't know.' He looked contemptuously at the engineer. 'Do you mean to say you kept watch all that time?'

Perkins smirked. 'I felt I had a duty.'

'You bloody little hypocrite,' Lycett said.

The smirk vanished from Perkins's face and he looked vicious. 'I don't have to take insults from you. I could call you worse names.'

'Possibly you could.' Lycett stood up. 'Don't bother to show me out. I can find my own way.'

'What are you going to do?'

Lycett stopped with his hand resting on the door-knob. 'Do?'

'About what I just told you. About her. About — them.'

'I don't think it's any of your business. I don't think it was any of your business right from the start.'

'But you'll do something? You can't just let things slide. You won't let them get away with it?'

Perkins seemed strangely insistent and Lycett wondered why. What was it to him? Perhaps he owed the mate a grudge and was using this roundabout way of getting his own back. It did not occur to Lycett that it might be the woman in the case who had earned Perkins's enmity.

Without bothering to answer, he opened the door and left the cabin. He was boiling with anger. It was not only Moira's infidelity that incensed him, but that fact that a louse like Perkins should have been the one to tell him about it. He felt a small degree of satisfaction for having beaten the engineer's head against the bulkhead, but he would have liked to beat the little wretch's brains out.

A thought came into his mind; suppose Perkins had been lying. He clutched at the possibility. She had said she had been with the Mensteins for part of the evening, and if that were true she could not have been in Johansen's cabin from nine fifteen to eleven forty-five; in which case Perkins must certainly have lied. Well, there was one way of finding out the truth about that. He would speak to the Mensteins.

\* \* \*

'There'd be no risk to it,' Grade said.

Holt stared at him. 'No risk! What if the customs blokes open the box and find it doesn't just hold tea? They're not fools, you know; they know the tricks.'

'So what if they do find the junk. Just tell 'em the truth.'

'That I was going to put a couple of

pounds of heroin on the market? They'll love that.'

'Not that truth. The other truth. That Saunders gave you the box to take to his partner; that you thought it was just China tea like he said.'

'And if they don't believe me, tell them to get in touch with Saunders for corroboration. Fine.'

Grade sighed. 'Don't be so gloomy, Nick. Take my word for it, nobody's going to dig inside that box. You look too innocent. Nobody'd suspect you of drug smuggling in a million years. Why do you think Saunders picked on you?'

'Customs are suspicious people. They're paid to be.'

'Are you going to throw away ten thousand pounds?'

'There's another point. It's not simply a case of breaking the law. It's immoral.'

'What's so immoral about it? It's just trade.'

'Helping people to become addicts. Giving them a push down the slope and getting rich out of it. That's what you call just trade?'

'Look, chum,' Grade sounded like a patient teacher explaining a simple proposition to a backward pupil, 'you aren't going to push anybody down the slope. There won't be one

146

extra addict just because you've put that stuff on the market. One way or another, the people that want a fix will get it, don't you worry. The only difference will be that you'll be that much worse off. Don't you want the money?'

'You bet I want the money.'

'Then take it, for Pete's sake; take it.'

Holt lay on his bunk and thought it over. Grade certainly had a point. Putting that parcel of heroin into circulation was not going to make any appreciable difference to the number of drug addicts. Sure, you could take the strictly moral attitude and have nothing to do with the traffic; you could throw away ten thousand pounds, which might be just what you needed to start your fortune. But why be such a fool? It was like stopping arms supplies to some country because they might be used for the wrong purpose. So what happened? You offended a would-be customer, someone else supplied the arms anyway, and you lost the profit. Such conduct benefited nobody except the rival arms suppliers. And they were laughing.

'Morals are for the missionaries,' Grade said.

The missionaries! Well, hadn't he, Nick Holt, set out from England as a kind of missionary? So what if he had? He had done

147

his share of helping his fellow men; now it was time he started thinking about himself. He had his own life to live and there was no job waiting for him in Australia now.

'You made your mind up yet?' Grade asked.

'I'll think about it,' Holt said.

★ ★ ★

Captain Leach looked at his chief officer with distaste. He did not like Johansen; he never had liked him and he did not suppose he ever would. Johansen was the kind of man who played around with other men's wives, and that was a subject regarding which Leach had good reason to feel bitter. Indeed, so deeply was the bitterness ingrained in him, that in a man like Johansen he was blinded to any possible good qualities by reason of that one outstanding vice. In the Dane Leach could see nothing good, nothing good at all.

For his part, Johansen regarded Leach as a drunken old fool. It seemed to him that he himself would have made a far more competent master of the ship, and he made little effort to disguise this belief from his superior. With such antagonism existing between the captain and the mate, there was little possibility of that co-operation which is vital to the smooth running of a ship. The *Chetwynd* had many handicaps: she was old, she was worn, she was neglected; but perhaps the greatest handicap of all was this lack of concord among her officers.

'Well?' Leach said. 'What is it, Mr. Johansen? I imagine you have not come to my quarters simply to pass the time of day?'

Leach felt sick in his stomach; his head ached; instead of a tongue he seemed to have a mouthful of tarred rope. Sometimes he wondered why he bothered to go on. It would be so easy to end it all; nothing to do but slip silently overboard on a dark night; no one to see him go, no one to mourn for him. Oblivion.

'I am not happy, Captain.'

'Great God!' Leach said. 'What do you expect me to do about that? I'm not happy. Sparks isn't happy. Who the devil is?'

Johansen controlled himself with an effort. He would so have liked to knock Leach down. 'It is the weather that makes me not happy.'

'It's too hot for you?'

'Is not that, Captain. I do not mind hotness. But I think mebbe we head for trouble.'

'Trouble! What d'you mean?'

'I think there is storm somewhere. I feel it.'

'So you feel it, do you?' Leach's voice was heavy with sarcasm. 'And have you any other evidence apart from this feeling?'

'The glass. It drop a little.'

'You don't have to tell me about the glass. I can read it for myself.'

Johansen wondered whether Leach had in fact looked at the barometer lately, whether he had not been too busy looking into another kind of glass. But he said nothing.

'You've read the weather reports that have been received on the radio, I imagine,' Leach said.

'I have.'

'Any mention there of storms?'

'No, Captain.'

'But you think your feelings are more reliable.'

'Mebbe the weather people get it wrong. Mebbe they make mistake.'

'So what do you want me to do?'

'You do what you damn please, Captain.' Johansen was beginning to lose his temper. 'I just tell you what I think. I don't tell you what to do. You feel like it, you turn this whole damn ship upside down. Not my bloody business.'

'Thank you, Mr. Johansen.' Leach's voice was icy. 'I think that will be all. Unless you have something more to tell me about your — feelings.'

'No, Captain. No more to say.' Johansen walked out of the cabin and only with difficulty refrained from slamming the door. So be it then. He had done his duty. Now let the Old Man do what he liked. He, Carl Johansen, washed his hands of the whole affair.

Alone in his cabin, Leach poured himself a glass of whisky and drank it slowly. He wondered whether there could be anything in the mate's hunch about the weather. But, damn it, there would have been something on the radio, and according to the reports Maggs had brought there had been no hint of anything untoward. Yet Johansen had said the glass was falling a little. Well, what if it was? There were bound to be slight variations in barometric pressure; that was nothing to worry about. If it fell rapidly, that would be a very different kettle of fish. But it was not falling rapidly.

Leach shrugged. Johansen was making something out of nothing. He could feel it indeed! Damned nonsense. Leach drained his whisky and poured another.

★ ★ ★

Lycett found the Mensteins sitting in deckchairs in the shade. They looked very small, sitting there, patiently waiting, as they had so often waited patiently in the past.

Lycett said, 'You don't like the sun?'

'The sun can be a little too hot,' Menstein said. 'Then it becomes oppressive.'

'Never too hot for my wife. She's a regular sunworshipper.'

'A very beautiful woman, Mrs. Lycett. More than once I am saying to Sara that it is so.'

Mrs. Menstein added her meed of praise for Moira Lycett, 'So elegant. So charming.'

'You and my wife are pretty good friends, I believe.'

'Good friends?' Sara Menstein seemed a little puzzled.

'She talks to you a lot.'

'Oh, no. We say 'Good morning' sometimes. But no, we do not talk a lot.'

Lycett did not care for the sound of it. Nevertheless, he pressed on. He had to be sure. 'But yesterday evening. You must have talked quite a bit with her then.'

Both Mensteins showed astonishment. 'Yesterday evening?' Menstein said. 'Why yesterday evening?'

'She was with you, wasn't she?'

'With us? Oh, no; you are mistaken.'

'We see Mrs. Lycett at dinner,' Sara

Menstein said. 'After that we do not see her again. Why do you think she is with us, Major?'

'A misunderstanding. Some remark I must have heard incorrectly. So you did not see her at all?'

'Not after dinner.' Sara Menstein looked worried. 'Is it important?'

Lycett made an attempt to appear unconcerned. It was a poor effort and he did not believe it deceived the Mensteins, who were both now watching him closely. 'Important? Oh, certainly not. Of no importance at all.'

He got away from them as quickly as he could, but he felt that they still watched him until he was out of sight. Why had he been stupid enough to approach them at all? He might have known what kind of answer he would get. And now he had as good as told two more people that Moira had deceived him. Damn her! And damn Johansen! They had been laughing at him, laughing. Perhaps the whole ship was laughing. He had to do something about it; by God, he had. And he would too. Maybe Johansen would find it was not quite so funny after all to take a man's wife right from under his very nose. Maybe he would find Morton Lycett a tougher proposition than he had bargained for; a hell of a lot tougher.

She was still asleep when he went into the cabin. She had a great capacity for sleep. She had only a sheet for covering and one of her bare, sun-tanned arms was hanging over the side of the bunk. Lycett put a hand on her shoulder and shook her none too gently, until she opened her eyes.

She stared up at him for a moment or two, as though unable at once to get him into focus. Then she said, 'What is it? Is something wrong?'

Lycett stood with his left hand resting on the upper bunk gazing down at her. Her hair was disarrayed and she did not look quite so elegantly attractive in this first awakening as she would later when she had done some work on her appearance. She looked more her age. But still voluptuous, still worthy of a man's attention. Oh, yes; no doubt at all about that.

'Should anything be wrong?'

'I don't know.' She sounded a shade petulant. 'Why did you wake me?'

'Haven't you had enough sleep?'

'Does it matter to you how much sleep I have?'

'It does when I want to talk to you.'

'You mean to say that's all you woke me

for?' She sat up and swept her hair back with an impatient movement of the hand. 'Give me a cigarette.'

He gave her one and lit it for her. He watched the smoke drift out of her mouth. 'You haven't asked me what I want to talk to you about.'

'What do you want to talk to me about?' Her tone was flat. She could not have been less interested.

'About where you were last night.'

'Oh, Lord!' she said. 'Do we have to go all through that again? I thought we'd had it out.'

'This time I want the truth.'

'You've had the truth.'

'You spent the evening with the Mensteins?'

'Yes.'

'That for a start is a lie. I asked them. They said they didn't see you again after dinner.'

She drew more smoke from the cigarette and regarded him coolly with those wonderful eyes that had once driven him nearly crazy, and perhaps still could. 'So you check up on me. Nice to have trusting husband.'

He gave a short, bitter laugh. 'Trust! I've got good reason to trust you.'

'All the same, you shouldn't have questioned the Mensteins. It could make you look silly.'

155

His voice rose a little. 'I don't care about looking silly. I just want the truth.'

She stared at him through the drifting tobacco smoke with a mixture of mockery and contempt, saying nothing. She despised him, and he knew it. The knowledge goaded him to fury. What right had she to despise him? He seized her by the arms and shook her as he had shaken Perkins. The cigarette fell from her mouth and began to burn a hole in the pillow-case.

'Answer me! Answer me! Where were you?'

She tried to free herself from his grip, but anger seemed to have given him added strength and her struggles were in vain. He continued to shake her from side to side.

'You were with Johansen, weren't you? Admit it. You were with him.'

'Yes,' she shouted. 'I was with him. And I'll be with him again tonight. Now are you satisfied?'

He stopped shaking her. He had known it. And yet, hearing it from her own lips could still come as a shock. Even to the end he had still entertained the thought that it might not have been true, that Perkins had been lying; but now there could no longer be any doubt. He had demanded the truth and he had got it.

He released her arms and slapped her on

the cheek. 'Whore!' He slapped her again. 'Bloody whore!'

She rolled over sideways and her bare shoulder touched the forgotten cigarette. She gave a cry of pain, slid off the bunk, stumbled and fell at Lycett's feet. He pushed her away from him with the sole of his shoe, then walked to the wash-basin and drew a glass of water from the tap. Pungent smoke was rising from the smouldering pillow. He poured the water on it and the fire went out with a hiss.

'You will not be with him again tonight,' Lycett said. 'You'll never be with him again. Never.'

# 7

## Message for Johansen

It was during his spell on the bridge in the dog watch that Mr. Johansen noticed the first really unmistakable signs of the approach of dirty weather. An airless, humid, sweaty heat hung over the ship and all the ironwork seemed to ooze moisture like the skin of a man sick with fever. And yet the sun was no longer shining completely unobscured as it had been earlier. There was a misty halo round it, as though water had been splashed on to its surface and the water had evaporated into steam.

A few high, feathery cirrus clouds strayed across the sky and gave it the bluey-white appearance of adulterated milk. There had been sea-birds with the ship that morning, diving for the garbage that Chin Kee threw overboard; now there were no birds; they had all fled, as though fearful of some imminent peril.

The mate consulted the barometer and saw that it had fallen again. He went out on to the port wing of the bridge and looked towards the north-east, away on the port quarter. From that direction the sea came rolling towards the ship in a long oily swell. The water no longer looked blue and limpid; it appeared thick and dirty, as though some mud had been stirred into it. Yet still there was no wind, no breath of air to ruffle the surface of the sea; only that oily swell making the ship roll a little as she steamed inevitably on.

Johansen sent for the radio officer. Maggs appeared, looking sullen.

'Still no report of storms, Mr. Maggs?'

'If there had been, I wouldn't have heard them,' Maggs said.

Johansen glanced at him sharply. 'How so?'

'The radio's not working. It's broken down.'

'So? But you mend it? You mend it damn quick?'

'Can't do. It's a transformer burnt out. No replacement. You know what this ship is?'

Johansen swore. He certainly did know what the ship was: old, decrepit, with worn-out equipment. And now the radio had broken down.

Nevertheless, to Johansen's way of thinking, there was something not quite right here. He looked at Maggs suspiciously. 'You say nothing this morning when I talk to you. You do not say then that radio is no good.'

'It was after that it broke down.'

'Why do you not report it at once?'

'I've been trying to get it right, haven't I?' Maggs sounded aggrieved. 'You don't suppose I've just been sitting on my backside doing nothing.'

Still it sounded wrong to Johansen. 'But before it break down, there is no report of bad weather?'

'I told you once. Nothing. Why do you keep asking?'

'Bad weather coming.'

'You feel it in your bones?' Maggs was sarcastic.

'More than my bones, Mr. Maggs. Look.' He pointed at the sky, at the sea.

'No wind,' Maggs said.

'Wind will come. Will come bloody strong, I think. Soon.'

'Well, that's your pigeon. Nothing I can do.'

He left the bridge exulting. He had caught them now. They were well and truly caught; all of them. And he had done it. He was so pleased with himself that he felt an urge to confide in someone, to boast of his cleverness. But he could not do that; he would have to keep it to himself. But it was worth it.

As the hours of Mr. Johansen's watch dragged away he liked the look of things less and less. He debated in his mind whether to call Captain Leach and suggest a change of course. But he remembered his earlier reception by the Old Man and he had no desire to risk a repetition of that unpleasantness. He had little expectation that Leach would come up to the bridge of his own accord; he scarcely ever did so in the mate's watch, preferring to have as little contact as possible with his second in command. And as he had expected, Leach did not appear.

But if Johansen did not call the captain, he did call the serang; and though it was already dark he gave orders for everything to be made secure, the hatch-covers checked and extra lashings put out, life-lines to be rigged between poop and midcastle and between midcastle and forecastle. The serang took these orders without comment and went away to see that they were carried out without delay.

Johansen looked again at the sky and did not like it.

★ ★ ★

Nick Holt noticed the unusual activity of the crew when he went on deck for a breath of fresh air. It was stifling in the cabin. He thought it so strange that he went straight back below and told Grade about it.

'It looks to me as if they're getting ready for a storm. They've even slung a heavy rope the whole length of the deck, both fore and aft.'

Grade digested this information. 'Certainly looks like they're getting ready for something. I had an idea the weather was changing. Too damned oppressive.'

'There's no wind.'

'No wind, maybe, but the sea's doing things. The old tub's beginning to toss a bit.'

'That's true. You think there is a storm coming, then?'

Grade shrugged. 'I'm no weather prophet, chum, but I'd say that when they start battening down and rigging life-lines at this time in the evening it isn't just for something to amuse themselves with. I'd guess that somebody thinks there's something nasty on the way.'

Holt felt a tremor of excitement. He had told Grade he had a wish to see what a real storm was like and he had meant it. He had been in ships in rough weather before, but

162

nothing really big. Perhaps this would be the big one.

'You ever been seasick?' Grade asked.

'Never. I've got a cast-iron stomach.'

'You're lucky, Nick boy. Me, I feel queasy already.'

★   ★   ★

Grade was not the only person feeling queasy. Moira Lycett was also an easy prey to seasickness, and as the *Chetwynd* began to react more and more to the movement of the sea, she felt the first unmistakable symptoms of that distressing malady. Her head ached; she felt no desire for food; even cigarettes nauseated her. She lay on her bunk listening to the creaking of the woodwork, uncomfortably aware of the slow rise and fall of the cabin floor and the seasaw action of the bunk itself, while the hot, bitter taste of bile rose in her throat and refused to be swallowed.

Lycett, himself immune, regarded her suffering without pity; indeed with no little satisfaction. In that condition she was hardly likely to have any desire to go to Johansen's cabin. It would not even be necessary to keep a watch on her. There was that to be said for seasickness: it very effectively killed the appetites; all of them.

Moira groaned. 'Why can't it keep still?'

'It'll be worse before long,' Lycett said complacently. 'Will you be taking dinner, my dear?'

She looked at him venomously. 'You're enjoying it, aren't you? You're glad I'm seasick.'

Lycett smiled. 'It does have a certain irony, you must admit. I don't imagine Johansen suffers from the same complaint. Though I believe Nelson did.'

'To hell with Nelson.'

'Could be where he is. I thought it might be some consolation to you to reflect that even our greatest naval hero suffered in exactly the same way as you are suffering now. And he couldn't just lie down under it. He had his duties to perform.'

'Damn you, Morton,' she said. 'Will you shut up.'

Since that outburst in the morning she had noticed a change in him, a rather puzzling change. He seemed to have become almost gay. She had seen that kind of mood in him before; it usually came on when he was planning something; and more often than not the something he was planning would be a way of swindling some luckless victim out of a quantity of money. But that could hardly be the reason for his gaiety now. Yet she felt sure

164

he had some scheme revolving in his mind; now and then she caught an inscrutable smile twisting his petulant little mouth; but she knew that in the present state of their relations it would have been useless to ask him what he was thinking about.

She had been surprised by the violence of his reaction to her confession. She had not thought him capable of so much passion. Was it because he loved her or was it simply hurt pride that had caused him to lash out like that? Difficult to say. She had been married to Morton for over twenty years and there were still sides to his character that she did not fully understand, and perhaps never would. She knew that he was dishonest, vain, self-centred and unreliable; now it seemed that he was also deeply jealous and capable of violence. But how much violence? That was the question. And she had to admit that she did not know the answer.

'You're very sensitive,' Lycett said with a suggestion of a sneer. 'And in your present state not, if you'll forgive my saying so, the best of company. In the circumstances I think I'll take a turn on deck.'

He went out of the cabin and left her to suffer alone.

* * *

165

Mr. Johansen noticed with a trace of malicious amusement that there were fewer passengers than usual at table for dinner. The Australian was absent, and so were the Mensteins. The absence of Moira Lycett amused him rather less. He had been looking forward to a repetition of the pleasures of the previous evening, but if she were seasick that seemed scarcely likely.

Lycett, however, was there. and Johansen made a polite inquiry about his wife. 'Not sick, I hope, Major.'

'Are you interested?' Lycett asked, giving him a penetrating glance.

'Always interested in the health of passengers.'

'Duty, eh?'

Johansen answered carefully, 'As you say, duty. But more than that. We take personal interest too.'

'In everyone?'

'Sure.' Johansen gave a laugh. 'If you are sick I am interested in you too, Major.'

'I am never sick,' Lycett said.

'You are lucky man.'

Lycett stabbed at a piece of meat with unusual viciousness, as though stabbing the heart of a mortal enemy. 'Yes, I am very lucky. I am never seasick and I have a beautiful, faithful wife. What more could one ask? Isn't there something in the Bible about a virtuous woman being a crown to her husband?' He turned to Sydney East, seated on his left. 'That's true, isn't it?'

East looked embarrassed. He muttered an agreement and turned his attention to the food on his plate.

'Of course it is,' Lycett said. 'You should know. You've got your crown here with you. Mine, unfortunately, is lying on her bunk suffering the agonies of seasickness. I fear she won't be venturing far this evening. No social life for her at all.' He looked hard at Johansen. 'That's what your ship has done for her. It rolls a little and Mrs. Lycett cancels all her engagements. Isn't that a pity?'

'A great pity,' Johansen agreed. He hoped Lycett would drop the subject. His remarks were becoming a shade too pointed. Johansen had a pretty thick skin but he did not go looking for unpleasantness; and a jealous husband was not quite what he would have ordered for dinner. He wondered, a trifle uneasily, just how much Lycett knew and how much he was guessing.

'She will not be keeping any appointments,' Lycett said. 'Always supposing she has made any.'

Johansen ignored the remark. He began to talk to Pearl East, and again it struck him how attractive she was. In the absence of Moira Lycett there was much to be said for this one. Less sophisticated perhaps, but what of that? She might be worth a little of his attention. And she did not appear unwilling to talk.

'Are we going to have bad weather, Mr. Johansen?'

The tableclothes had been damped to stop plates and glasses from sliding, but if the movement of the ship became more pronounced even this precaution would not be enough and the fiddles along the edges of the tables would have to be raised.

'Nothing to worry about,' Johansen said. 'Mebbe a pocket of wind come. Mebbe rain too.'

'You would have warning of any bad storms over the wireless of course.'

'Of course,' Johansen said, and looked for Maggs; but Maggs was also absent. Perhaps he too was feeling a little sick. Unless he was working on that radio.

'And there has been nothing?'

Johansen smiled at her. 'Nothing. You are not alarmed?'

'I am always nervous when the ship starts to roll,' she confessed. 'The sea can be so frightening. It's so big, so deep. Like a great monster just waiting to swallow you up.' She looked at the mate, met the full impact of his pale blue eyes, read something there that she did not wish to read, and dropped her gaze, abashed. 'That sounds very silly, I expect.'

Johansen was gallant; he was enjoying these exchanges more than those he had had with Lycett. 'No, not silly. Sea is a monster. Sure. But we fight him. You bet we fight that old damn sea. Trust us, Mrs. East. We don't let no harm come to our lovely passengers.'

Sydney East seemed about to say something, thought better of it and remained silent. But he did not look pleased. Mr. Johansen's heavy gallantry was obviously not to his taste, much as it might appeal to a feminine audience.

It was Lycett, however, who broke in softly, 'And if your own life were in danger, would the passengers still come first, Mr. Johansen?'

Johansen did not answer for a few moments. Then he said: 'Is no need, I think, to talk of such things, Major. No lives are in danger. Not now. Not at any time. No.'

Lycett took a sip of water and put the glass down carefully on the damp cloth. 'But that,' he said, 'is what we don't know, isn't it?'

Johansen stared hard at Lycett for a while, but Lycett stared serenely back, and in the end it was the mate who dropped his gaze.

He was angry with himself. In a way he felt as though he had suffered a defeat.

* * *

Saul Menstein was not seasick, but Sara was and he would not leave her. It was so silly of him, she thought; and yet so touching.

'You must go and eat your dinner,' she said. 'What need is there for you to stay with me? I am only a little sick. Because I do not feel like eating, is that any reason why you should starve?'

He took her hand. 'It will not hurt me to go without a meal. I am eating too much. Soon I shall be fat. I must watch my waistline.' He released her hand and patted his stomach. 'So expensive if I have to buy new suits.'

She smiled. The idea of Saul growing fat was too fantastic. Why, he was nothing but skin and bone; a breath of wind would have blown him away. It was as though the starvation of the concentration camps had put its mark on him for ever. On her also.

'I wish you would go, Saul.'

But he was adamant. 'No. I stay here with you. There was a time when I could not be with you.' She saw his eyes cloud with the memory of that period in their lives, and this time it was she who pressed his hand. 'So do not scold me, Sara, if I refuse to leave you now.'

She smiled at him, feeling a wave of tenderness for him. It was surely worth a little sickness to know that he still loved her so dearly.

★  ★  ★

Johansen left the dining saloon just ahead of Lycett. Lycett overtook him in the alleyway.

'I have a message for you, Mr. Johansen.'

Johansen stopped. He turned and faced Lycett. 'Message? What message?'

'Do not wait up.'

'You speak in riddles. I do not understand. Explain the meaning please.' Johansen spoke impatiently. He was getting somewhat tired of this fat, pompous man who was so obviously jealous and so obviously impotent to do anything about it.

'The meaning is that tonight you will not have company.'

'That is the message? Nothing more?' There was a mocking note in Johansen's voice. His smile was mocking.

Lycett was suddenly goaded beyond endurance. That this man who had seduced his wife should now have the presumption to laugh at him to his face. 'You bloody bastard!'

He took a swing at Johansen with his right fist, and the very unexpectedness of the action took the mate off guard. Lycett's fist struck him on the side of the mouth, smashing his lips painfully against his teeth.

This was too much for Johansen's self-control; he lost his temper and hit back at his attacker. The mate's blow was considerably heavier than Lycett's; it struck him on the chest and flung him back against the side of the alleyway; his head made violent contact with a fire extinguisher in an iron bracket and he slid to the deck, feeling dazed, angry and sick.

Johansen, whose lips were bleeding slightly on the inside, might have worked off his spite by giving Lycett a bit more punishment if Holt and Perkins had not at that moment appeared on the scene.

Holt stared at the fallen Lycett in astonishment. 'Hello, what's happened here?'

Lycett pointed an accusing finger at the mate. 'That swine hit me.'

Holt glanced at Johansen. 'Why did you do that?'

Johansen dabbed at his lips with a handkerchief. 'Is he attack me first. I just hit back. Self-defence.'

'Pretty strong self defence,' Perkins said. He seemed to be enjoying the situation. 'I don't think you ought to treat a passenger like that. You could be in trouble, Mr. Johansen; you surely could.'

Johansen turned on him. 'You shut your damn trap. Is not your business.'

Perkins stepped smartly back, as though fearing that the mate might be about to treat him in the same way as he had treated Lycett. 'Okay. So it may be none of my business. But I still say you ought to watch it.'

Johansen still seemed in half a mind to have a go at Perkins, but the little engineer had prudently taken refuge behind Holt, and he thought better of it. He turned abruptly and strode off down the alleyway.

Lycett called after him savagely, 'You won't get away with this, Johansen. I'll make you pay. You'll be sorry you ever crossed swords with me. I'm warning you, you'd better look out. You've asked for it and you'll get it.'

He was still spitting out threats even after the mate had disappeared from view.

Holt and Perkins helped him to his feet, and Perkins said insinuatingly, 'I reckon you owe him more now, Major. First that other business, now this. Oh, yes, I'd say you really do owe him something now.'

But Lycett snarled at him, 'Shut up, you sneaking little rat. I don't want your opinion.' He brushed Perkins's hand from his arm and also walked away, lurching slightly as the ship rolled.

'There's gratitude for you,' Perkins said. 'After all I've done for him.'

★ ★ ★

On the bridge Mr. Finch was feeling uneasy. He knew that dirty weather was on the way. Even if Mr. Johansen had not told him so, he would have guessed it for himself. You needed no weather reports to tell you that the glass was falling; and there was that nasty oily swell running, which made the ship roll and plunge; there was something evil and menacing about that.

The sounds of the crew driving wedges securely home on the hatch coamings did nothing to allay his uneasiness. If Mr. Johansen thought it necessary to have tasks like that carried out at this hour he must be expecting more than a mere squall, considerably more. Finch had not had a very wide experience of storms at sea, but he had had enough to give him a healthy respect for what the forces of nature could do to a ship, and even indeed a certain amount of fear. Oh God, he thought, as if I didn't have enough on my mind already!

And there was another thing: Captain

174

Leach had not put in an appearance on the bridge since the watch began. In the ordinary way Finch would have regarded this as a blessing, but in the present circumstances he would have welcomed the reassurance of Leach's presence. Drunken old boozer though he might be, Leach had had vast experience; he had seen it all, been through it all. Finch feared and hated Leach, but in an emergency there was no man in whom he would have had greater confidence. So why did he not now make his usual visit to the bridge and lend the third mate the moral support of his authority? Mr. Finch could not help thinking that it was sheer cussedness on the part of Captain Leach that was keeping him away.

'Damn him!' Finch muttered. 'Damn him, damn him!'

And then he felt the first touch of wind on his face, warm and damp, like some giant's breath flowing over him. He heard the halyards shiver as if with apprehension.

# 8

## Bit of a Nut Case

Mr. Johansen, after leaving Lycett, made his way to Captain Leach's cabin. He was reluctant to do so after his earlier rebuff, but having turned matters over in his mind, he had finally decided that there were certain things Leach ought to know; one of which was that the radio was out of action.

Of course it was possible that Maggs had already reported this to the captain, but there could be no harm in making sure. It might be as well also to report what precautions he, Johansen, had already taken.

The door of Leach's cabin was shut. Johansen rapped with his knuckles and waited. There was no answer. Johansen knocked again, again listened, his ear close to the door. From within he thought he could detect a faint sound, a sound that rose and fell with monotonous regularity. There had been no invitation to enter, but Johansen decided to take the invitation for granted. He turned the knob, pushed open the door and walked in.

He noticed at once the reek of spirits. The ship leaned over to starboard and a bottle, still with a little whisky swilling around inside it, rolled towards him and stopped at his feet. The mate braced himself against the slope of the deck and gazed round the cabin. His eyes discovered Leach at once; the captain was lying on the settee, snoring heavily. It was this snoring that Johansen had heard from outside.

Johansen walked to the settee. 'Captain,' he said. 'Wake up, Captain.' And then more loudly: 'Wake up, damn your guts!'

Leach did not stir. He was wearing drill trousers and a drill shirt, both garments crumpled and stained. His feet were bare and he was lying half on his side and half on his stomach, with one leg hanging over the side of the settee and touching the floor. Johansen gripped his shoulder and shook him. The snoring altered in pitch, rose to a kind of gurgle as if the man were choking on his own saliva, then returned to normal. Leach's eyes did not open; it was like shaking someone under an anaesthetic. He was dead drunk and it would take more than shaking to bring him back to consciousness. Johansen saw the futility of what he was doing and stepped back.

'Okay then, Captain. You sleep. You sleep

damn good. Mebbe you never wake up no more. Mebbe damn good you don't.'

He turned and went out of the cabin. The bottle rolled in pursuit and almost caught him before the ship returned to an even keel; then it began to roll back the other way. Johansen closed the door gently behind him.

* * *

She was just passing the door of his cabin when he arrived there. And seeing her, the idea leaped into his head. With the storm coming, with Captain Leach drugged with alcohol and himself in virtual command of the ship, there would be a certain piquancy in the situation. Her presence there at that moment was in a way providential, making up for the absence of the other woman; it would be flying in the face of fortune to neglect the opportunity. And why was she there anyway? This was not a part of the ship that she would normally frequent. So perhaps she had come for a purpose. He was vain enough to believe that he could guess her motive.

He gave his charming smile, ignoring the slight pain of the cut lips. 'Mrs. East. You wished to see me?'

She looked embarrassed, like a child caught out in some escapade. Johansen thought the confusion added to her attractiveness. Maybe she was a better bargain than the other one; maybe she was at that.

'I think I've come the wrong way.' she said. 'I wanted to change this book at the ship's library.' He saw now that there was a book in her hand. She gave a nervous laugh. 'I ought to know my way round this ship by now.'

'No need to go to the library,' Johansen said. 'I got plenty books. Novels.' He pushed open the cabin door and switched on the light. 'Take what you please, Mrs. East. I got better books than library.'

She seemed reluctant to enter the cabin. She drew back a pace. 'Oh, no, Mr. Johansen. There's no need to bother you. And I must return this book.'

'Is no bother,' Johansen said. 'And I return book for you.' Before she could stop him he had taken the book from her hand and had a grip on her arm, light but firm, the charming smile still making him look young and boyish. 'Come; I show you my library.'

She made a half-hearted attempt at refusal, but his hand still gripped her arm and he had the book that she had been taking back to the ship's library; and after all what harm could there be in borrowing one of his books? It would have seemed so silly to refuse.

He noticed her indecision and increased

179

the pressure on her arm. They always wanted to have their minds made up for them, and he was the man to do just that. 'I have a book I think you like. Romantic. Come.'

She allowed herself to be persuaded into the cabin. Johansen followed her in and closed the door.

'You like this cabin?'

She glanced quickly round it. 'It's very nice. Where are the books?'

Johansen ignored the question. 'Is small mebbe. You think is too small?'

'No. Not really. I mean — '

Johansen threw the library book down on the table on one side of the cabin. 'Big enough for one man, you think? Mebbe big enough for one man and one woman?' He laughed, indicating that it was a joke.

She did not echo his laughter. She was feeling uneasy. If Johansen had not been standing between her and the door she might have walked out there and then. But she would have had to push past him and he was a big man.

'The books, Mr. Johansen.'

'Carl. Call me Carl.'

She was silent.

'Go on. Say it.'

She said slowly, 'The books — Carl.'

Johansen snapped his fingers. 'Good, good.

Is not so hard to say. Now what I call you? Not Mrs. East. Too formal. You and me, friends. So, I call you by first name too. What is your first name?'

She hesitated, then answered with some reluctance, 'Pearl.'

'Pearl! That is fine. It suit you. You are a pearl. A perfect pearl.'

'The books,' she said again, trying to bring him back to the subject. 'You said you had some books.'

'Books. Yes, sure. Plenty books.' He opened a locker, took out a handful of paperback novels and spread them out on the table. 'You choose.'

She glanced at them. The covers were frankly sexy, near-pornographic. The titles indicated the kind of literature that appealed to Johansen's taste.

'I don't think this is quite what I'm looking for.'

'Sure. Everyone looking for this. You, me, everyone.'

She became aware of his arm round her waist, pulling her towards him. He was grinning.

'No,' she said. 'No, Mr. Johansen.'

'Carl.'

'No, Carl.'

'Yes, Pearl.'

She tried to free herself from his grip, but now his other arm was round her and he was too strong. He began to kiss her. She struggled but she felt weak; his arms were crushing her and his mouth was moving, questing.

'No! Oh, no!'

The ship rolled. It caught both of them off balance and they fell together on to the bunk. She could feel the hard edge of the side-board grinding into her waist. Johansen's hands were moving, fumbling at her dress.

She screamed. One of his hands clamped down on her mouth. She heard his voice and could detect the excitement in it, the roused desire.

'Quiet. I don't hurt you. You like it too. Don't be fool. Now you be quiet, huh?'

The hand eased from her mouth and she bit it with all the strength of her jaws. Johansen gave a cry of pain and anger, and then he seemed to go berserk. He hit her once, twice. On the second blow she lost consciousness.

★ ★ ★

When she regained her senses she was lying on the bunk and Johansen was sitting on a chair watching her. He had a glass of gin in his hand and there was a little blood on the hand where her teeth had sunk into it.

'You awake now? Good.' There was a note of relief in his voice, though he seemed to make an attempt to conceal it.

She sat up and her head felt like lead and there was a stiffness about her jaw. She held her head in both hands and gave a moan.

'You remember what happen?' Johansen asked.

She looked at him with contempt and loathing. 'I remember.'

'The ship roll. You fall and hit your head on table. Knock you out.'

So that was to be his story. She looked at her dress. It was torn. Was the fall supposed to have done that also?

Johansen followed the direction of her glance. 'You catch the dress too. Pity. Nice dress. Mebbe you mend it, huh?'

She got off the bunk, steadying herself with a hand as the ship rolled. She looked at Johansen. There was no doubt that he was worried. Perhaps he had never intended to go so far, but had lost control of himself. Perhaps he had expected to meet nothing more than token resistance, misled by past easy seductions. He was looking back at her covertly, possibly calculating what his chances were of getting away with this story. She

183

noticed that the paperbacks had been cleared from the table.

'You do remember falling, Mrs. East?'

So it was back to Mrs. East, not Pearl any more. Did he really believe that his blows had obliterated her memory? Was that the straw at which he was clutching?

'I remember.'

He seemed to breathe a little more easily. 'Such accidents will happen.'

'You have had an accident too, I think, Mr. Johansen.'

'I?'

'Your hand.'

She moved unsteadily to the door, opened it and left the cabin. As she walked away she heard the sound of breaking glass. Johansen had thrown his tumbler on the floor.

★   ★   ★

Moira was still lying on her bunk when Lycett returned to the cabin. He scarcely glanced at her. He went straight to the wash-basin, soaked a flannel in water and pressed it to the bruise on his head which had resulted from contact with the fire extinguisher. The spot felt tender and there was already a swelling. What he really needed was some ice; the water was tepid rather than cold.

Moira turned on her side and looked at him. 'What's the matter with you?'

He answered savagely, 'Nothing's the matter with me. Mind your own business.'

'Have you knocked your head on something?'

'If you must know, yes. On a fire extinguisher.'

'How on earth did you manage that? Have you been drinking too much?'

He turned and snarled at her, 'No, I haven't been drinking too much. It was your lover boy. Johansen.'

She looked surprised. 'He hit you? Why?'

'Because I hit him first. Split his lip.'

'Well,' she said, 'you do ask for trouble, don't you, Morton?'

'He's the one who's asking for trouble. And he's the one who'll get it. You bet your sweet life he will. He needn't think he can play his little games with me. I'm not taking it, see. I'm not going to be made to look a fool.'

'You're making yourself look a fool,' she said irritably. This wretched seasickness and now his playing the idiot over that Johansen affair. Who would have expected him to make such a fuss? 'Why don't you let it drop?'

'Let it drop!' He moved over to the bunk and stood looking down at her, the flannel pressed to his throbbing head. 'I suppose

185

that's what you'd like. You don't want him to get hurt, do you? That's what it is — you're afraid he might get hurt. Your fancy man.'

'Don't be such a clown, Morton. I'm not bothered about him. He can take care of himself. If anyone is going to get hurt, it's likely to be you.'

'And that wouldn't bother you either, would it? Clown, eh? We'll see who's a clown. I think you underestimate me, my dear. You may be in for a surprise; a very big surprise.'

She stared up at him through the nausea of seasickness. It was just talk of course. He would never do anything. Hitting Johansen in the teeth and getting slammed for his pains was about as far as he would go. That was his limit.

And yet, could she be so sure? She had never seen him quite so roused. Perhaps when you reached his age it was even more necessary to assert yourself than it was in youth. Perhaps you held on more tenaciously to what you had and lashed out more blindly at any rival. Could he really be contemplating something violent — even criminal?

'You'll see,' Lycett said. 'You'll see.'

★  ★  ★

'It's getting rougher,' Menstein said. 'There seems to be a wind rising.' He walked to the open porthole and peered out at the blackness of the night. A few drops of spray were flung in and he could taste the salt on his lips. 'I think I had better close this.' He swung the plate glass in its hinged brass frame across the opening and tightened the wing-nuts.

Sara watched him from her bunk. Even to that simple task he seemed to bring a delicate skill, handling the brass nuts as he might have handled forceps or a scalpel.

'Do you think there is going to be a storm, Saul?'

He turned slowly. He had to control himself because he was afraid, and he must not let her see that he was afraid. Yet he could not suppress his fear. He did not think he was a coward; in fact he was sure that he was not; he had faced torture and worse with fortitude. But the sea still had this power to frighten him. It was something he could not explain; something born in him.

'No; it is nothing. A squall perhaps. It will have passed by morning.'

He heard a wave break against the side of the ship; he heard the timbers complaining. Pray heaven it might be so. But he was still afraid.

Holt was telling Grade about Lycett's encounter with Johansen. He thought it might take Grade's mind off his seasickness.

'You mean he actually hit Johansen in the mouth?' Grade said. 'I didn't think he had the guts. What triggered him off?'

'I don't know. When I got there Johansen had already knocked him down.'

'Not difficult to guess what the argument was about. Ten to one the luscious Moira came into it.'

'You think Lycett is jealous?'

Grade swallowed some bile and managed to grin in spite of it. 'Jealous as they come. I've had some talks with our Major and I know. If I were Johansen I'd watch my step.'

'You're not telling me you think Lycett would do anything really desperate?'

'For that woman,' Grade said, 'I think he'd commit murder.'

On the bridge Mr. Finch was feeling more and more uneasy as the hours of his watch passed. The wind was strengthening; no doubt about that; and the sea was beginning to toss the ship about quite a lot. And still

Captain Leach had not put in an appearance.

Finch could not keep still. He walked into the chartroom, had a look at the charts, came out again, glanced over the helmsman's shoulder at the compass, peered out through the wheelhouse windows and could see very little, went out on to the port wing, came back, went through it all again. Now and then he thought about the girl who might be making love to other men in Hong Kong.

He was thinking about her when the radio officer appeared on the bridge.

'There's going to be a storm,' Maggs said.

'So you got a report at last?'

'No, I didn't. I can see for myself, can't I? I can read the signs as well as the next man. It's going to be bad. Oh, yes, real bad.' There was an exulting note in Maggs's voice that puzzled Finch. There seemed to be no reason for it.

'I can't understand why there's been no warning on the radio.'

'Well, there may have been, mayn't there? We wouldn't hear it.'

'Why not?'

'Didn't the mate tell you? Radio's fallen by the wayside. Gone on strike.'

'You mean it's out of action?'

'That's it.'

'Mr. Johansen didn't tell me.' Finch

sounded aggrieved. Did the mate think it was of no interest to him?

'Well, you know now.'

'Can't you repair it?'

'D'you think I haven't tried? You can't make bricks without straw.'

'Can't you transmit either?'

'No.'

'So you couldn't send out a distress signal?'

'Now why should we want to do that?' Maggs asked.

'It could happen.'

'Oh, yes, it could happen. We could be in a lot of distress. But from now on, Finchy, we're like the bird with B.O. — we're on our own.'

Finch could not for the life of him understand why Maggs sounded so happy about it. It was as though he were taking a personal delight in the situation and contemplating with intense satisfaction the possibility that the ship might be in need of assistance and unable to send out a Mayday call.

Sometimes Finch wondered whether Maggs was not a bit of a nut case, he really did.

★ ★ ★

Lycett's mind was in a ferment as he stepped out on deck. He hoped that the fresh air would clear his head, help him to decide what to do. One thing he could not do in his present state was climb into his bunk and sleep. Sleep! He wondered whether he would ever sleep soundly again.

The air that met him was like a warm, damp blanket; it was so saturated with moisture that everything he touched was wet. He walked to the after end of the promenade deck and leaned on the rail, staring down at the shadowy deck below. He had a sudden urge to go to the poop where he could see a light shining. It was as though he felt the need to put as much distance as possible between himself and his problem.

Johansen! What malicious fate had ordained that that man should be thrown in his path? Well, was it not the way things had always gone for him? Nothing had ever turned out well. Even when he had thought himself on to a good thing, it was all a deception; he was just being led on to the inevitable crash. He had been an unlucky devil — always.

He walked to the head of the ladder leading down to the afterdeck. He went down backwards with one hand on each rail, carefully, the ship doing its best to throw him off. When he reached the foot of the ladder he turned and saw that a thick rope stretched away aft at about shoulder height, disappearing into the gloom. He had never noticed this rope before and he could only conclude that it had been rigged up because bad weather was expected. Even now it would be a help in crossing the afterdeck.

He gripped the rope with his right hand and began to walk aft along the shifting deck. He was wearing rubber-soled shoes and the wet iron was slippery underfoot; he would certainly have fallen had it not been for the life-line.

When he came to the gap between the hatches he found that the rope had a thinner line attached to it; this line ran off at right angles and was made fast to the mainmast, taking up the slack. The ship rolled so heavily at that moment that water slopped over the bulwarks and rushed across the deck before gurgling away down the scuppers. Lycett hung on with both hands and felt the water flowing over his ankles. Then he went on.

There were some dim lights in the after-castle but no sounds of life came from the crew's quarters. Lycett went up the ladder to the poop and walked to the stern. He could hear the thumping of the propellor and the sound of churning water like the flow through a millrace, and looking down he could see the white foam of the wake fanning out astern.

He leaned on the taffrail and the foam below seemed to hypnotise him. He could not drag his eyes away. He leaned out further and yet further; the thunder of the churning water roared in his ears and seemed to fill his head, beating, beating, like a million drums.

Suddenly he knew that he was falling. He turned half over as he fell and hit the water with his back. The shock of it cleared his brain, but it was too late. He began to struggle, but the stream carried him away, away into the impenetrable darkness of the night.

No one had seen him fall; no one had heard his despairing cries for help. The ship went on and left him.

# 9

## Middle Watch

Finch was glad when Mr. Prior relieved him at midnight. By then Finch knew that there was something really bad coming. In the north the stars had been completely blotted out by a black mass of cloud, illuminated now and then by flickers of lightning. Finch could hear the distant rumbling of thunder and another sound that he found both puzzling and disturbing, like a kind of wailing and moaning. He experienced a tingling in his spine and his scalp prickled, as though he had heard the weird voices of banshees.

Ned Prior came like an answer to a prayer. There was something so sane, so earthy about him, something indeed so fatherly, that Finch felt immediately reassured by the mere presence of the older man.

'Well now,' Prior said, 'it doesn't look too healthy, does it, Finch me lad?'

'It looks nasty.' Finch said.

'Did we have any warning of this over the magical wireless waves?'

Finch told him what Maggs had said and

Prior shook his head. 'Pity, pity. Still, it can't be helped. How's the glass behaving?'

'Dropping fast. Faster than I've ever seen it drop.'

'I see. Has the Old Man been up during your watch?'

'Not a sign of him.' Finch proceeded to air his grievance. 'Other nights he'd be up, plaguing the life out of me. But tonight, when he's really wanted, no.'

'In that case it might not be a bad idea to tip him the wink when you go down.' Prior paused a moment, then added, 'On second thoughts, maybe it'd be better to see the mate. Let him break the good news to our dear captain.'

Finch also thought that it might be a better idea; he had no wish to inform Captain Leach that there was a storm coming up and that he ought to be taking a bit of interest in it. He might get some curses for waking Mr. Johansen, but he would rather face a disgruntled mate than an irate captain. He hurried away on his errand and left Mr. Prior to the duties of the watch.

★ ★ ★

Finch rapped on the door of the mate's cabin and waited. There was no answer, no

195

invitation to enter. Finch rapped again. Still no answer. He supposed Johansen must be sound asleep, but then he noticed that there was light showing under the door and it seemed strange that the mate should have gone to sleep without switching the light off. Mr. Finch gave one more rap with his knuckles and then opened the door.

He was quite prepared to be yelled at, to be cursed, to be told to get to hell out of it; there would have been nothing unusual in that. But he was not prepared for what he was to find when he walked into the cabin; and he wished it could have been someone else and not he whose ill fortune it had been to stumble on what was waiting inside.

Mr. Johansen was lying on the floor of the cabin. He was lying face upwards and his eyes were open. But the eyes did not move; they had a glassy look about them and they were staring straight up at the deckhead, as though intent on something up there, something not apparent to anyone else.

'Mr. Johansen!' Finch said in a low voice. 'Mr. Johansen!'

Johansen took no notice of the third mate, did not even glance at him. And now Finch noticed something else: there was broken glass on the floor, the chair was overturned and broken, the table was hanging askew, the bedding had been half-pulled off the bunk, and the door of the wardrobe was open and swinging. Some articles of clothing had spilled out of the wardrobe and were scattered about the cabin.

Finch was no detective, but it needed no great powers of deduction to reach the conclusion that a desperate struggle had taken place in the cabin. And if further evidence were needed there was the wide, deep gash in Johansen's forehead, and the blood.

Finch felt sick, but he forced himself to kneel down and take the mate's left wrist in his fingers, feeling for the pulse. He could detect no sign of any beating. He let the arm fall; it was still quite flexible; therefore Johansen could not have been dead long enough for rigor mortis to set in. And then, as Finch kneeled, the ship rolled so heavily that Johansen's head fell over to the left, bringing the eyes into line with Finch's own.

This was too much for Mr. Finch's nerves. With a cry of horror he jumped up and made for the door.

★   ★   ★

Nick Holt was finding sleep elusive. The porthole had had to be closed and it was stiflingly hot in the cabin. The ship was rolling so heavily now that the bunk was like a seesaw, one moment your feet were up in the air, the next moment they were down. How could any man sleep in such conditions? And in the lower bunk Grade was as sick as a dog.

Holt decided to give up the search for sleep and take a look at the weather on deck. He switched on the light over his bunk, swung his legs over the side, waited for the ship to come back to an even keel and dropped to the floor.

Grade was also awake. He said, 'What are you up to?'

'Can't sleep,' Holt said. 'Going to take a turn on deck.'

'Looks like you're getting your storm. Been whistling?'

'No. It came without my help.'

'If I thought you were to blame I'd strangle you.'

Holt was pulling on his trousers. 'You feel bad?'

'My back teeth are under water and I've got a head like a church bell — with the clapper going.'

'Want me to get you anything?'

'Like one made-to-measure coffin?'

'You won't die. Unless the ship goes down.'

'Right now,' Grade said, 'that might be the lesser evil.'

Holt left him to his misery and went out of the cabin. It was past midnight and there was a different character about the interior of the ship at this time of night; the alleyways were deserted and it was as though all the human element had vanished, leaving the vessel to go on by itself with its monstrous heart thumping below and all its bones creaking in agony. Holt had intended going straight up on deck, but now he had a curious impulse first to explore the interior, to see what it looked like at this hour when everyone but the watch-keepers had retired.

He went first to the dining saloon. It was dark in there. He found the switch and turned the lights on. The fans had stopped and two of the chairs had fallen over. There was a stale odour of food and cigar smoke, close and oppressive. He noticed that all the portholes had been closed and screwed tight. He heard glasses clinking.

He switched the lights off, left the saloon and closed the door behind him. He had taken no more than two paces when Mr. Finch crashed into him. There was a wild, terror-stricken look in Finch's eyes and for the moment he seemed not to recognise Holt.

Holt said, 'You're in a hurry, Mr. Finch. Where's the fire?'

Finch stared at him. 'Fire? What fire?'

'It was just a joke. You seemed to be in a great hurry to get somewhere.'

'Did I?' Finch seemed dazed. He put a hand to his forehead. 'Where was I going?'

'I don't know.' Holt wondered whether Finch was ill. And then it occurred to him that Finch must have had some kind of a shock. 'Has something happened?'

'Happened,' Finch repeated. Then he seemed to get a grip on himself. 'Yes, something has happened. Something terrible. Mr. Johansen has been murdered.'

'Murdered!'

'He's lying in his cabin. Dead.' Finch gripped Holt's arm and shook it. 'Do you understand? Dead.'

Holt understood. And something that Grade had said flashed into his mind, 'For that woman I think he'd commit murder.' Grade had been talking about Morton Lycett.

'What are you going to do, Mr. Finch?'

'I — ' Finch seemed to have no idea what to do.

'You'd better tell the captain.'

'Yes,' Finch said. He sounded grateful for the suggestion. 'Yes, that's what I must do. I'll go and tell him now.'

He released Holt's arm and walked away. Holt also walked away — in the direction of the mate's cabin.

Mr. Finch had been in such a hurry to escape that he had not even closed the door. When Holt arrived he found it swinging. He hooked it back, then bent down and examined the body lying on the floor. It did not take him long to convince himself that Finch had been right: Mr. Johansen was undoubtedly dead.

Holt glanced round the cabin and saw the disorder, and he came to the same conclusion that Finch had reached: Johansen had not died without a struggle. He wondered what Lycett had used for a weapon; he must have had something; that gash in Johansen's forehead indicated as much; and anyway, a man of Lycett's physique would hardly have been able to overpower the husky mate with the aid of nothing more than his bare hands. Holt looked for something that might have filled the bill, but he could see nothing. Well, of course, Lycett was not likely to leave it lying there; he would get rid of it at once. And there would be no difficulty about that; the sea would swallow up any evidence of that kind and no one would ever find it.

But was he not jumping to conclusions? He had no proof that Lycett had been the murderer, and until suspicion was changed to certainty he ought to keep an open mind. Very well then, he would keep an open mind, difficult though it might be with everything pointing to Lycett as the killer.

Holt wondered why Finch was taking so long in fetching Captain Leach. They should have been here by now. Perhaps he ought to go and see whether Finch had in fact gone for Leach; the third mate had looked pretty shocked and it was possible that he was just wandering around in a daze.

Then Holt's eye was caught by something on the cabin floor; a small silvery object lying partly hidden by the body of the mate. He had not noticed it before, and in fact it was only the rolling of the ship, shifting the body slightly, that revealed it now. Holt bent down and picked it up, looked at it for some time, deep in thought, then dropped it into his pocket.

★   ★   ★

The reason why Finch was such a long time was that he was having difficulty in rousing Captain Leach. Leach was still snoring, as he had been when Johansen had left him some four hours earlier. The only difference was in his position: he was now lying flat on his back on the cabin carpet, having apparently been tipped off the settee by the movement of the ship. When this had happened it was impossible to say, but it had obviously not been a sufficient jolt to waken him; or if it had been, he had decided to go to sleep again where he was and not bother to climb back on to the settee.

Finch shook him, shouting, 'Captain Leach! Wake up! Captain! Wake up!'

Johansen had tried the same treatment with the same lack of success that Finch was having now. Leach snored on. In desperation Finch went to the captain's bathroom and drew a tumbler of cold water. He carried the tumbler to where Leach was lying, hesitated a moment, appalled by his own temerity, then flung the water in his captain's face.

Leach's mouth was open and a quantity of the water went into it and down his throat. The snoring ceased abruptly and was replaced by such a horrible gurgling noise that the terrified Finch wondered whether he had succeeded in doing nothing more useful than choke the life out of another man. Then Leach's eyes opened, focused on Finch with the tumbler still in his hand as evidence of his guilt, and glowered balefully.

Finch trembled.

Leach sat up suddenly and uttered a long drawn out growl that sounded to Finch like 'Gaaarroogh!' and made him tremble even more violently. He tried to say something but his tongue would not form the words. He just stood there, holding the empty tumbler and shaking from head to foot.

'Mr. Finch,' Leach said in a thick, cold, deadly voice. 'Did you throw water over me?'

Finch answered in a high-pitched squeak: 'Yes, sir.'

Leach began to get up from the floor. Finch darted forward to help him, but Leach brushed the proffered hand aside with a curse. He got to his feet, staggered a little and sat down heavily on the settee. Again he glowered at Finch.

'No doubt you've got an explanation. You'd better have. It'd better be good.'

'Mr. Johansen has been murdered, sir,' Finch said.

If he had been expecting some violent reaction to this revelation he was to be disappointed. Leach did not reel back in horror; he did not even give a jerk of the head. Not by any movement or gesture or change of expression did he give a hint that the words had touched any nerve. He merely stared back at the third mate in silence.

Finch wondered whether the fact had sunk into Leach's drink-sodden brain or whether the fumes of alcohol had made it impossible for him to assimilate such information. With his voice rising shrilly he repeated the statement.

'Mr. Johansen has been murdered. Do you understand, sir?'

'I understand,' Leach said. 'Where is he?'

'In his cabin. What are you going to do, sir? Oh God, what are you going to do?'

'Don't get bloody hysterical,' Leach said. 'Bring me my shoes.'

Finch found the shoes, brought them to Leach, helped him to put them on. He smelt the alcoholic reek of Leach's breath and the sweaty reek of his shirt.

'You're sure he's dead, Mr. Finch?'

'Oh, yes, sir. No doubt about that,' Finch said, and had a sudden vision of the mate, returned to consciousness and walking about. What would Leach say then? But it could not be. He was really dead.

They both became aware of the sound at the same time. It was like a wild shrieking. The ship staggered, as though struck by a blow.

'Wind,' Leach said.

'Yes, sir. It's a storm coming up. It looks bad, sir. I was going to tell Mr. Johansen, but — '

'You've told me,' Leach said.

He got to his feet, lurched a little, walked to the bathroom, relieved himself, then doused his head with water. He washed out his mouth and stared in the mirror at the sagging, unshaven face, the lank strands of hair, the bloodshot eyes.

'Bartholomew,' he croaked, 'you're a bloody beauty and no mistake.' He walked back into the cabin and rejoined the waiting third mate. 'Come on, Mr. Finch. Let's go and look at him.'

★ ★ ★

Holt was still waiting in Johansen's cabin, as though standing guard over the body. He was surprised by Leach's personal appearance. Leach had not even bothered to comb his hair, and his shirt was soaked with water. He looked like a man suffering from the father and mother of all hangovers.

He glanced momentarily at Holt, then looked down at Johansen. 'This is how you found him, Mr. Finch?'

'Yes, sir.'

'One of you had better fetch Dr. Menstein. Not that he can do much. Too late for that.'

'I'll go,' said Holt.

★ ★ ★

Menstein was not asleep and he came at once. He confirmed what was only too apparent: Mr. Johansen was undoubtedly dead, having died most probably from the blow that had inflicted the gash in his head. Menstein did something that no one else had seen fit to do: he closed Johansen's eyes.

'Do you know who did this thing?'

'We do not,' Leach said.

Holt became aware suddenly that Perkins had appeared on the scene. He was standing in the cabin doorway, looking in.

'I could make a guess at that,' Perkins said.

They all turned and stared at him, and he gave a smirk, as if he enjoyed being the centre of attention.

'Do you know something?' Leach asked.

'I know Mr. Johansen and Major Lycett had a fight earlier this evening. I know Mr. Johansen knocked the major down and the major threatened to get even with him.' Perkins cast a meaning glance on the body on the floor. 'Looks like he did too.'

'You actually heard Lycett threaten Johansen?'

'You can say that again. Mr. Holt heard him too. He was there.'

Leach glanced at Holt. 'Is that so?'

Holt admitted that it was.

'What was the quarrel about?'

Holt did not answer, but Perkins gave a grin. 'About Mrs. Lycett. What else? She was in this cabin till near midnight yesterday evening.'

'How do you know that?' Leach asked sharply.

'I don't go about with my eyes shut.'

'You mean you spied on Mrs. Lycett?'

'I wouldn't call it that.' Perkins sounded sulky.

'God knows what you would call it then. And no doubt you felt it your duty to inform Major Lycett?'

'Yes, I did. It wasn't right, what the mate was doing.'

Captain Leach looked at the engineer as one might look at something loathsome discovered under a stone. 'Mr. Perkins,' he said flintily, 'I should be obliged if you would take yourself as far away from me as possible. It is too much to expect that I shall never see you again but one can but hope, one can but hope.'

Perkins went red in the face. 'All right, I'll go. But I'm telling you, if you want to find the man who killed the mate, you look for Major Lycett. He can't be far away.' And with that he turned from the doorway and disappeared.

'That man,' Leach said, 'ought to have been drowned at birth.'

Menstein was pulling nervously at his left ear. 'All the same, there may be something in what he said. Indeed I very much fear so. Major Lycett was checking up this morning — that is yesterday morning — on Mrs. Lycett's movements. He seemed to be under the impression that she spent the previous evening with my wife and me. We had to tell him it was not so. He seemed rather upset.'

'I think Major Lycett had better be found.' Leach said.

★ ★ ★

But that was to prove more easily said than done. A visit to his cabin by Mr. Finch revealed that he was not there. Moira Lycett, lying awake in her bunk, demanded, not without reason, why her husband was being sought at that time of night. It was an embarrassing question. Finch stammered and said that he had better start getting back to his duties. Nothing could have been better calculated to rouse her suspicions that something was afoot. Already she had been more than a little worried by Morton's absence; usually he was in his bunk and asleep long before that.

'Something has happened, hasn't it, Mr. Finch?'

209

'Well — ' Finch said.

She sat up, her head aching, and the cabin seemed to revolve. Some of the movement was real; Finch put out a hand to steady himself.

'You had better tell me,' she said. 'I'm bound to hear eventually.'

Finch had to admit to himself that she had a point. The facts could not be kept secret. She would have to know.

'Mr. Johansen has been found dead in his cabin. It looks as if he was murdered.'

Her eyes widened with horror. 'Oh, no, no.'

'I'm afraid so.'

'And you think Morton did it?'

Mr. Finch felt extremely uncomfortable. It was, of course, precisely what he did think, but one could hardly admit such a suspicion to Mrs. Lycett. One could hardly give one's reasons for thinking her husband a murderer. Not to her.

'We should just like to know where he is.'

'He's not in here. You can see that.' She was wondering whether Morton could really have been such a fool. And she feared that it was only too probable, remembering the temper he had been in. With sudden clarity she saw what this was going to mean; the publicity, the sordid facts of her relations with the dead man coming out at the trial;

everything. Oh, why had she ever gone to Johansen? Why, why, why? But for that one visit to his cabin, none of this would have happened. Now she was going to be punished, and the punishment would be out of all proportion to the crime — if crime it was. In taking his revenge on Johansen Morton could not have succeeded in taking a more complete revenge on her also. It was all so unfair, so horribly unfair.

'When did you see him last?' Finch asked.

'When?' She put a hand to her throbbing head. 'Oh, after dinner. He came back here. He'd been — ' She stopped. She had been about to add that he had been fighting with Johansen, but decided not to. They probably knew anyway; someone was bound to have seen the fight.

'When did he go out again, Mrs. Lycett?'

She frowned, trying to remember. 'Oh, an hour later perhaps. About a quarter to ten. I'm not sure.'

'And he hasn't been back since?'

'No.'

Mr. Finch moved to the door. 'We shall have to find him.'

He had not reached the door when the sound halted him. It was the wind certainly, but such a wind as he had never heard, had never thought or hoped to hear. It was a sound to freeze the blood, to make even the boldest heart miss a beat. Mr. Finch's heart was not one of the boldest; it missed more than a beat and his lips trembled.

'My God! Listen to that!'

And then it seemed that a monstrous fist had slammed the side of the ship, making it shiver and heel over to starboard. Finch could not save himself; he was thrown forward and fell across the bunk on which Moira Lycett was lying. With his face buried in the soft, warm folds of her bosom, he heard the sound of rushing water.

# 10

## Never Singly

Mr. Prior, peering through the wheelhouse window on the port side into the howling darkness, caught a glimpse of the great wave coming. It was like a moving ridge of granite, snow-capped where the crest was broken into foam. The wind came in with the wave, and wave and wind struck the *Chetwynd* together, struck her hard, so that she staggered and groaned under the blow, so that she heeled over and took the seas over her bulwarks, took them on her foredeck and her afterdeck in a mass of swirling, turbulent water.

The wind persisted, and Mr. Prior, staggering like the ship, holding on, bracing his arms and legs against the strain, knew it . for what it was, the hurricane wind whirling round the edges of the storm. It was this that he and Mr. Finch had heard in the distance at the start of the watch; but now it was magnified beyond all imagining; shrieking, buffeting, tearing at every rope and cable and canvas with maniac fury, and driving the waves like sheep before it.

And now the rain came too; came not apparently in separate drops but in a single blinding sheet of water, cascading like some torrent spouting from a fissure in the sky. The wind caught it and flung it almost horizontally against the wheelhouse windows, mingling it with the salt spray and the foam whipped from the waves. And with this rain came an ever-increasing weight of darkness, split momentarily time and time again by jagged flashes of lightning. There was thunder too, but the thunder simply mingled with the general din, even its growlings and rumblings somehow rendered insignificant in comparison with the mighty anger of the wind and the sea.

'My word!' Prior muttered. 'This is something. This is really something indeed.' And it occurred to him to wonder whether the poor old *Chetwynd* was a good enough ship to get through such a storm, whether she had not perhaps come at last to the end of her sea-going days.

But he did not allow his thoughts to dwell for long on that bleak possibility. He clawed his way across the wheelhouse to the engine-room telegraph and rang for half ahead. The ship was pitching and tossing as well as rolling heavily, and possibly the propellor would be coming clear of the water as the stern rose. Prior sighed. It was all a great nuisance, upsetting the normal uneventful course of things. Some people might say it made a nice change, but Prior was far too old to desire any such change; all he wanted was to finish his time at sea as peacefully as possible and retire to a little pig farm with what savings he had been able to put away and any pension that he might be fortunate enough to get. But one could not order the weather.

He caught a glance from the helmsman. The man was standing with his feet wide apart, thin hands gripping the wheel, lips compressed. Prior thought he detected a question in the glance; doubt; perhaps fear also. This small dark man of a different race, a different background, was looking to him for reassurance. Perhaps somewhere he had a wife, children, waiting for his return.

'It's all right,' Prior said gruffly. 'All right.' And hoped it might be.

$$\star \quad \star \quad \star$$

Mr. Finch lifted his face from Moira Lycett's breasts and stood up, holding on to the upper bunk for support.

'I'm sorry. I didn't mean to do that. I was

215

taken off balance.'

She gave no indication that she had even noticed what he was saying. She was listening to the other sounds, the much more fearsome sounds that came from outside, like an enraged monster furiously striving to break in.

'It's getting worse, isn't it? Much worse.' She seemed for the moment to have forgotten the errand that had brought the young third mate to her cabin. 'The ship might — ' She hesitated, as though fearful of putting the awful possibility into words.

Finch saw that she was afraid. 'The ship is not in any danger,' he said, striving to put into his voice that confidence which he did not altogether feel. 'No danger at all.'

Moira Lycett gripped his free hand. 'Are you sure? Quite sure?'

'Yes,' Finch said, 'I am sure.' But he knew that it was a lie. He was not sure at all. How could he be sure? Ships could sink even in these days in certain conditions. The conditions were right for sinking the *Chetwynd*.

He said, 'I must go.'

She gripped his hand more tightly. 'Don't leave me. I'm afraid. Stay with me.'

'I can't.' It occurred to him that it was perhaps not quite decorous to be there at all.

Moira Lycett was lightly clad to say the least. His nervous glance rested for a moment on certain aspects of her body and shied away. 'Yes, I must go.'

He drew his hand away from hers, went out of the cabin and closed the door. He felt sorry for the woman; she was sick, she was afraid, and now there was this other ordeal that she would have to face. But there was nothing he could do for her. Nothing.

He supposed he ought still to be looking for Major Lycett, but where to look? He was still turning this question over in his mind when he saw the serang. The serang was wearing an oilskin coat which glistened with water; water dripped from him on to the alleyway floor. He stood in front of Finch, gripping the handrail, and began to speak rapidly.

'Sir, there is a man injured. He fall from bunk, hit head on iron, cut open. Much blood, sir, very much blood. This man is bad. Unconscious, sir. Must have doctor very quick.'

'We don't carry a doctor.'

'No ship's doctor, no. But there is a little passenger, sir; he is doctor. He will come.'

'Dr. Menstein!' Finch could hardly imagine him crossing that afterdeck in such a storm; he would be swept away. He shook

217

his head. 'How do you expect him to get to the poop?'

The serang answered earnestly, 'You help him, sir.'

'I?' The prospect of crossing that deck filled Mr. Finch himself with terror. Even inside the accommodation he could hear the seas that were sweeping over the bulwarks. 'I?'

'Yes, you, sir. Matter of life and death, sir. Hurry, sir. Fetch little doctor. Hurry.' He turned away. 'I go back now, sir. You come quickly.' In a moment he was gone.

Finch groaned. Here was another responsibility. For a moment he thought of doing nothing, simply ignoring the serang's request. But he knew that he could not do that; it would all come out later and then he would be in trouble. He decided to go for Menstein; perhaps the little doctor would refuse to go and that would let him out. Yes, almost certainly Menstein would refuse.

He found Menstein and Holt about to leave the mate's cabin. They had lifted Mr. Johansen's body on to the bunk and covered it with a sheet. For the present there was little else they could do. Captain Leach had gone away; he had other duties pressing upon him now.

'Have you found the major?' Holt asked.

Finch told him that he had not. 'He's not

in his cabin. Hasn't been in since before ten.'

'Well, he can't get away.'

'Something else has cropped up,' Finch said. He told them about the injured seaman. 'Of course you don't have to go to him, Dr. Menstein. Frankly, I don't know whether you could get across the afterdeck in this sea.' He was giving Menstein every opportunity to refuse.

Menstein looked as though he wanted to do just that. 'It is a terrible night,' he said, and he tilted his head a little on one side, listening to the fearful sounds of the storm. 'Is it possible to cross the deck?'

'The serang must have managed,' Holt said.

'The serang is an experienced seaman,' Finch pointed out.

'You could help Dr. Menstein.'

Finch stammered slightly. 'I couldn't guarantee his safety.'

'A man is badly injured. His life could be in danger.'

'Dr. Menstein's life could be in danger.'

'It is for him to decide.'

'I will go,' Menstein said, and he squared his narrow shoulders and drew himself up like a man facing his inescapable duty.

Finch gave a sigh of resignation. 'Very well. I'll get you an oilskin coat.'

'I'll come too,' Holt said. 'You may need an extra hand.'

Finch stared at him in disbelief. 'You? Do you mean you're volunteering to go out there?'

Holt grinned. 'I always did want to see a real storm.'

★　★　★

The wheelhouse door opened. A man came in. The door slammed shut, driven by a great gust of wind and rain. Mr. Prior recognised the new arrival as Captain Leach and he was glad to see him. Things were becoming altogether too unpleasant for the second mate's taste.

Leach stood for a few seconds just inside the wheelhouse, hanging on and breathing heavily, water dripping from his sou'wester and oilskins. When he had got his breath back he said, 'What course are we on, Mr. Prior?'

Prior told him, shouting to make himself heard above the racket. Leach directed him to alter it by thirty degrees to starboard, bringing the ship on to a more westerly course.

'We shall have the wind more on our beam then.' Prior objected.

'It'll take us away from the centre of the

storm. Give the order.'

Prior gave the order with some misgivings and heard it repeated by the helmsman. He did not follow Leach's reasoning, but Leach had given all the explanation he was likely to give and his was the final word.

Leach himself was not absolutely certain that his judgement was correct, but he had a picture of the storm in his mind, of winds revolving clockwise round a still centre, the eye; but in the eye a mass of turbulent water, no place for a ship. Judging by the direction of the wind he believed they were on the western fringes of the storm, which would undoubtedly be travelling southward. Therefore, the farther west he could bring his ship the better it would be.

He wondered why there had been no warning. Cyclones, willy-willies, call them what you would, did not spring up in a moment; their course was known by the weather men; ships were informed over the radio.

'Was there no broadcast report of this, Mr. Prior?'

'None. The radio is out of action.'

Leach, his head aching with the hangover, his tongue dry, thought of Maggs. The radio could not have been out of action for more than twenty-four hours; not as long as that.

Maggs had brought weather reports earlier; no hint in them of cyclonic storms. And there should have been. Had Maggs suppressed the information, given false reports? On the face of it, it seemed unlikely. What reason could there be for him to do so? What did he stand to gain?

He dismissed the question from his mind; there were other matters calling for his attention. Whether Maggs had or had not falsified the reports made no difference now; the storm was there; it had to be fought.

He started to move towards the binnacle, and as he did so a white monster reared up in front of the wheelhouse and crashed down upon it with terrible force. The windows shattered under the weight of water and the helmsman staggered back screaming, his face slashed by splinters of flying glass.

★   ★   ★

It was the monstrous shrieking of the wind that impressed Holt most when they stepped out from the midships accommodation and began the perilous crossing to the poop. He had said that he wanted to see what a real storm was like, and there could be no doubt that this was indeed a real one. There was lightning, there was thunder, there was rain, there were great waves like snow-capped mountains in the night; but it was the wind that filled him with awe. He would not have believed that there could be such a wind; it was like an invisible battering-ram, bludgeoning body and mind; it drove the rain and the spray before it, lashing the men as if with a whip.

They clung to the rails at the head of the ladder leading down to the afterdeck, and Menstein seemed to become even smaller, shrinking into himself.

'We cannot do it.'

Holt could scarcely catch the words for the din, but he guessed what the little doctor was saying. He tried to encourage him. 'They've fixed a rope down there. Just hold on to the rope. Mr. Finch will lead the way.'

Finch seemed not at all keen to do that, but Holt urged him on, and he went down the ladder backwards, clinging on tightly with both hands.

'Now you, doctor,' Holt shouted.

In the sudden glare of lightning he caught a glimpse of Menstein's face turned to him and saw the fear that Menstein could not disguise. He put a hand on the other man's shoulder. 'It's all right. Just hold on. I'll be right behind you.'

Menstein, like a man walking into his own

private hell, began to descend the ladder and Holt followed. Holt was carrying the medical kit tied up in a waterproof bag and slung by a cord over his shoulder, and he could feel the wind tugging at it as though intent on tearing it from him. Ten seconds later all three of them were clinging to the lifeline.

The ship seemed to be moving in half a dozen different planes at the same time. She was rocked by the wind, tossed this way and that by the mountainous seas, lifted, dropped, turned on her axis like the board of a seesaw, and never for a single moment allowed to have any rest, any respite from the ferocious battering. A cork could not have been treated more contemptuously, could not with greater ease have been flung from one wave to the next.

'Come on,' Finch shouted, his voice almost drowned by the tumult. 'Come on now.'

They began to move along the rope, and seas came over the bulwarks, thundering down on the deck, washing over the hatches, swirling round the winches, and engulfing the men to the waist, even to the armpits. Holt heard Menstein utter a cry of despair; one of Menstein's hands had been torn from its grip on the rope; he could not hold on against such a pressure of water; he had not enough strength.

Holt saw what was happening. He stretched out an arm and got it round Menstein's chest, supporting him, feeling wildly exhilarated by this battle with the elements, so that fear had no part of him. He would beat the sea and the wind; he would get Menstein to his goal if it was the last thing he did.

And he did get him there. They came to the shelter of the poop and went in, dripping sea water like men rescued from drowning. Finch slammed the door behind them and the sound of the storm was muffled; now it mingled with the creaking and rattling of the after-castle, with all those innumerable internal noises that told of the life and death struggle of the hard-pressed ship. The atmosphere was oppressive, full of thick odours — oil and paint, spices and sweat.

The serang was there waiting for them, other men behind him; dark faces staring out of the poorly-lighted background of the narrow, crowded alleyway; many voices chattering in a language unintelligible to the Europeans; chattering in excitement and perhaps also fear.

Finch spoke to the serang, striving to keep his voice calm. 'The doctor is here. Where is the injured man?'

'In there, sir.' The serang gave a jerk of his

head towards a door on his right. 'But there is more trouble. sir.'

'What trouble?'

'See.' The serang held out his right arm and they could see the blood dripping from a wound. 'The man is mad, sir. He is waked up and now he is mad. The pain in his head perhaps. He draw a knife suddenly. Start to attack us.'

Finch looked worried. Another problem. 'Is he alone in there?'

'Oh, yes, sir. We leave quickly. Lock the door.'

They heard a sudden wailing cry from the other side of the door. It sounded more like a wild beast than a human being.

'You must go in and overpower him,' Finch said; but he sounded doubtful.

The serang looked unhappy. 'He will kill, sir. He is mad.'

'But something has got to be done.'

Holt could see that Finch really did not know what to do. It was a difficult situation. Perhaps Mr. Finch was wishing that Johansen were still alive and had the handling of it. Perhaps Johansen would have gone in and dealt with the crazy seaman; but Finch was hardly the man for that task.

Surprisingly, it was Menstein who spoke in a calm, controlled voice. 'I will go in.'

'You!' Holt said.

Menstein gave a wry little smile. 'It is what I came for. I did not cross that deck for pleasure.'

'But suppose this man attacks you?'

'That is a risk I must take. Please open the bag.'

Holt took the bag from his shoulder and untied the lashing. Inside the bag was a small leather case, quite dry. Menstein opened the case and took out a hypodermic syringe.

'This will calm him.'

'If you can get it into him.'

'I can only try.'

'I'll come with you,' Holt said.

Menstein looked at him. 'You are not afraid?'

'Yes. But I will come.'

'I also am afraid,' Menstein said. 'But one must do what one has to do.'

'That's three of us then,' Finch said. He turned to the serang. 'Give me the key.'

The serang handed it to him. Finch unlocked the door. They went inside.

There were half a dozen bunks, double-tiered, and the reek inside was almost overpowering. Between the bunks was a long, narrow table, screwed to the floor. At the far end of the table, with his left hand resting on

227

it and the bloodstained knife still gripped in the other, was the crazy seaman.

He was bigger than most of the lascars and he was naked except for a pair of cotton shorts. He was thin and very dark, and his ribs were all visible under the skin of the chest. He had stopped screaming, but he was snarling like an animal cornered by hunters; his upper lip was curled back and his teeth were clamped tight, jawbones bulging and the tendons in his neck standing out like stretched cords.

He looked as though he had been half scalped; a flap of skin and hair was hanging down over his left ear, and above this flap the head looked raw and bloody. When he had regained consciousness it must have been an awakening to such agony that it had driven him to strike out blindly, at the serang, at anyone who might come in his way. Holt could almost imagine that he saw the tortured brain pulsing just below the surface of the blood-spattered skull.

And Menstein began to talk.

Holt could not understand what it was that Menstein was saying. It could have been Polish or even Hebrew. It just went on, gently, soothingly. The seaman stared at him, eyes wild with pain. Menstein moved forward, reached the end of the table, facing the man across its length. Holt and Finch followed him warily.

Menstein gripped the edge of the table, steadying himself as the ship bucked. They could hear the rudder chains rattling, the groaning of the timbers. Menstein talked on.

He began to advance along one side of the table. The seaman had not moved.

Menstein was within six feet of the lascar when he switched to English. He said, 'Drop the knife.'

The seaman appeared to understand, for he glanced down at the knife in his hand. But he did not drop it.

Menstein edged a little closer. 'Drop the knife now.'

And suddenly the man began to scream. It was a terrible sound. His mouth just went wide and the scream came bubbling up from his throat. The scream seemed hardly to belong to him; it was like the voice of a devil coming out of a man possessed.

Menstein stopped moving and looked at the knife. The blade was nine inches long, tapering to a point. It looked razor-sharp and there was blood all along the edge.

Menstein said for the third time, 'Drop the knife.'

The lascar stopped screaming suddenly. He came round the end of the table and went for

Menstein, the knife raised above his shoulder.

'Oh, my God!' Finch cried.

The knife descended in a glitter of bright steel. But, amazingly, Menstein was not there. At the last moment he had moved aside and the knife passed by him, burying its point in the wood of the table.

'Now!' Holt yelled. 'Get him!'

He and Finch jumped at the lascar and bore him to the floor. He was struggling and screaming madly, but they held him there. Menstein stepped forward, plunged the needle into his arm, and in a few moments he was still.

'Now,' Menstein said, 'to work.'

★   ★   ★

When they came out of the after-castle the storm had not abated in the least, but Menstein no longer seemed afraid.

'We have crossed once,' he said. 'I know that it is possible. Let us go back. My wife will be worrying.'

Sara was awake when he went in. She took his hands in both of her own. 'Saul. Oh, Saul. I have been afraid, so afraid.'

He smiled at her. 'I, too, Sara. I, too, have been afraid. But I think perhaps never again. No, never again.'

230

* * *

The wheelhouse was awash with water; broken glass was everywhere. Mr. Prior had seized the wheel, but the helmsman was not as badly injured as they had feared; he had screamed perhaps more from shock and fright than from pain. After a while he came back to the wheel, possibly a little ashamed of himself, and insisted on taking over. Prior was not sorry to be relieved of his unaccustomed task.

Leach said, 'We've been nicely caught this time.'

'Mr. Johansen had an idea something was coming. He told Finch.'

Leach, remembering that Johansen had also informed him and had received no thanks from him for doing so, was not pleased to be told about the mate's forebodings by Mr. Prior. He answered somewhat sourly, 'Mr. Johansen won't be having any more ideas. Not in this world. He's dead.'

'Dead!' Prior was shocked. 'How? When?'

'He was murdered. By that Lycett fellow, I shouldn't wonder. They'd had a quarrel.'

Mr. Prior was just reflecting that troubles undoubtedly never came singly when, as though to emphasise the truth of this, the engines failed.

# 11

## On the House

The breakdown of the *Chetwynd*'s engines was something that Mr. Henderson had been predicting with monotonous regularity for more than a year. What they needed, according to that gentleman, was a major overhaul, or, better still, complete replacement with new machinery. But the directors of the Barling-Orient Line were strangely reluctant in the matter of major overhauls, and as for putting new machinery in a ship as old as the *Chetwynd*, that was quite out of the question. The Barling-Orient expected its engineers to make do and mend. Economy was the password, but there comes a time when a too rigid adherence to economy can lead to disaster. That time appeared to have arrived for the steamship *Chetwynd*.

Not that this would be likely to cause any great distress for the directors of the Barling-Orient, none of whom was on board the ship. If the *Chetwynd* foundered there would be insurance money to draw in compensation, and another ship could always be picked up cheaply to replace the one that had been lost. A pity if lives should be lost too, of course, but people who put to sea in ships must know that they took their lives in their hands. Barling-Orient could not be expected to control the weather.

When Captain Leach rang down to the engine-room to find out what the trouble was he got Henderson himself on the wire. The chief engineer had been there for more than two hours. What with the storm and what with his abiding worry about the engines, he had found it impossible to sleep and had finally come to the conclusion that he might as well do some work as lie sleepless on a wildly tossing bunk. His presence near the machinery had, however, not had any magical effect; the machinery had broken down in outright defiance of its appointed lord and master.

Captain Leach shouted into the telephone, 'What's wrong down there? What's happened?'

He found some difficulty in hearing the answer above the racket of the storm, and it was doubtful whether he would have understood the technicalities anyway. There was something about overheated bearings, cracked metal, and a lot of other meaningless jargon liberally interlarded with curses. He cut short Henderson's flow of language with the really important question.

'Can you fix it?'

What sounded like a derisive laugh rattled the earpiece. 'Fix it! There is no hope o' that. I warned you. I warned the owners. There comes a time of retribution. I'm telling you, Captain — '

Leach did not wait to hear what Henderson was telling him. He hung up the telephone and felt the vessel shudder. He heard Prior's voice.

'What's the verdict?'

'Bad, Mr. Prior. Very bad.'

'No chance of getting the engines going again quickly?'

'None.'

'Then we'd better say our prayers.'

Leach knew what Prior meant. The ship had been in enough danger even under power; now she was helpless, a plaything for the wind and the waves. And all their lives depended on the survival of the ship, for in such conditions there was no possibility of launching the boats; and even if launched, no boat could live in that boiling cauldron of a sea.

He noticed that the helmsman was still clinging to the wheel although there was now no steerage away. With the propellor no longer turning, the rudder was no better than a useless slab of metal hanging from the stern.

'If we had had warning,' he said. 'we could have avoided this.'

Prior made no comment. Leach turned and faced him. 'You think I'm to blame, don't you? That's what you think.'

'I don't think so.'

'Then you're either a fool or a liar. I am to blame. I should have known.'

'I blame no one,' Prior said. 'It's the will of God.'

'I don't believe in God.'

Lightning streaked across the sky, revealing in its white-hot glare the expanse of tormented water. The invisible wind screamed in insane fury.

'At times like this,' Prior said. 'I cannot help believing in God. Or the Devil.'

★ ★ ★

Finch decided to go and see whether Lycett had returned to his cabin. He found Moira Lycett still alone and distraught with terror.

'The major hasn't come back then?'

'No. No one has been here since you left me.' She noticed his drenched condition; he was dripping water on to the cabin floor.

'You've been out on deck? You've been looking for him there?'

'I've been on deck, but not to look for him. One of the seamen has been injured. I had to take Dr. Menstein to the poop to attend to him.' He felt rather proud of himself. It had been an ordeal at the time, but now it was something to look back on with satisfaction. He had proved equal to the the test. He chose to forget how nearly he had come to refusing to go.

She said, 'It's bad, isn't it? It's very bad.'

'It's not good,' Finch admitted.

He could see the fear in her eyes. 'We are in danger. We are.'

'No, Mrs. Lycett. You've got to get that idea out of your head.'

'I can't,' she said. 'I'm afraid.'

The cabin rose, leaned over at an angle and seemed to go sliding down into a pit. Moira Lycett gripped the side of the bunk and gave a cry of horror. The cabin stopped falling and began to move in another direction.

'Oh God!' she moaned. 'Oh, God, help me!'

Finch put his hand on her arm. 'Listen.'

She was silent, staring up at him, waiting for some new revelation of disaster. Finch waited for a moment or two in order to make

236

quite certain, but there could be no doubt about it.

'The engines have stopped.'

★ ★ ★

Grade noticed it too. Holt was changing his clothes, getting into something drier.

Grade said. 'Now we are in trouble. Real trouble.'

'Unless the engineers can fix things.'

'You ever tried fixing engines in a ship dancing about like this?'

'I'm not an engineer.'

'And engineers aren't miracle men. You ask my opinion, chum, we're all for the high jump.'

'Now you're being gloomy. It's the seasickness.'

'It is not the seasickness. I'm just using my head, and my head says when the engines of an old tub like this go crook in a storm like this you don't have a first class formula for survival. You're not A1 at Lloyds, if you get me.'

Holt thought Grade could well be right. It was not a pleasant thought. He was young and he had no wish to die; there was too much in life to look forward to. But other men had died young, countless millions of them, not wishing to do so. Death had no respect for man's wishes.

'Ships don't sink that easily,' he said.

'If the sea gets into them, they sink. Suppose some of those hatch-covers get ripped off and the sea gets into the holds. Just one hold. What then?'

'No reason to think the hatch-covers will be ripped off.' He did not wish to think about such things, and he wished Grade had not mentioned it.

'They could be though,' Grade said. 'You bet your boots they could be, chum.'

He seemed to be in a very gloomy mood indeed, Holt thought. Well, maybe it was the seasickness.

'Forty thousand dollars' worth of heroin,' Grade said. 'And it's never going to get to the customers. Hell.'

★ ★ ★

Leach and Prior were both surprised when they saw Maggs clawing his way into the wheelhouse. They were even more surprised when Maggs announced that he had repaired the radio.

'Do you want me to send out a distress signal, sir?'

Maggs had in fact done nothing whatever

238

in the way of repairing the radio for the simple reason that the apparatus had never been in need of repair. The truth of the matter was that, having by the suppression of the storm warnings brought the *Chetwynd* to her present perilous situation, he had now become thoroughly alarmed. He had never imagined that any storm could be quite so appalling, and now that death seemed to be more than a mere possibility he discovered, rather belatedly, that he had after all no great wish to die. He feared he might have left it too late to avoid that unfortunate outcome, but there was perhaps still a small chance of averting utter disaster, and he had to clutch at that chance, slender though it might be.

It came into Leach's mind that this was the first time he had seen Maggs since that disgraceful episode in his cabin when he had struck the radio officer with his fist. He ought never to have done that; he had lost his temper. Unfortunate. Most unfortunate.

Just how unfortunate it had been for the entire ship he had no way of knowing. Only Maggs could have told him that, and he was not likely to reveal the secret.

'I had the devil's own job putting it right,' Maggs said. 'But I managed.'

'Good for you, Sparks,' Prior said.

Leach added a grudging word of commendation. Perhaps he had misjudged Maggs. At least the man had not given up. He had probably been sweating away at that radio for hours.

'Yes, we'd better send out a signal. Come into the chartroom and take it down.'

\* \* \*

'Damn this for a game of soldiers,' Grade said. 'I need a drink. If I'm going to drown I may as well drown happy.'

'I thought you were seasick,' Holt said.

'Somebody once told me there's nothing like brandy for seasickness. Can't remember who it was, but somebody.' He climbed out of his bunk and began to dress while the cabin behaved like a cake-walk.

Holt sat on the lower bunk and watched Grade dressing. It was quite a performance; Grade fell over four times in putting his trousers on; but he finally succeeded.

'You coming, Nick boy?'

'The bar will be closed.' Holt glanced at his wrist-watch. 'Do you realise it's half-past four in the morning?'

'This is an emergency, chum. If the bar isn't open we open it. Are you coming?'

Holt got up from the bunk. 'All right. The

240

drinks are on you.'

'The drinks are on the house, chum, on the house.'

Grade opened the cabin door and a rush of water came in, swilling across the floor. The alleyway was a river with the current flowing first one way, then the other.

'This is nice,' Grade said. 'I just hope it hasn't got into the brandy.'

They clawed their way along the alleyway, clinging to the handrails. From the passengers' bathroom came a noise like somebody going berserk with a sledge-hammer in an ironmonger's shop. The water came sometimes up to their ankles, sometimes almost to their knees. Holt wondered where it had got in and whether there would be more.

They went up a short stairway, turned right and came to the door of the lounge. They went in. The lounge was very small; there were a few chairs and tables and a compact little bar on the left. The chairs had all fallen over, but the tables were screwed down and immovable. Lights were on and the Eurasian chief steward, Dai Jones, was behind the bar, as though he had been expecting them. He had a glass in his hand. The glass was half full of rum and it looked as if Jones was also.

He welcomed Grade and Holt with a wave of the glass. 'Come in, gentlemen, come in.

241

What can I get you? We have a most fine selection of liquors. Oh, indeed yes. Most fine.' With a magnificent sweeping gesture he indicated the bottles in their racks, and almost fell over, only saving himself by dropping the glass and clutching with both hands at the mahogany bar counter.

'Gimme a brandy,' Grade said. 'The biggest you've got.'

'Brandy, sir? Yes, indeed, sir. In one moment.' Jones made a grab at the brandy bottle, missed and fell down behind the bar. He made one or two futile attempts to get up and then apparently came to the conclusion that it was really not worth the effort. 'Good night, gentlemen. Good night, good sirs. Good — ' He closed his eyes and began to snore.

Grade lifted the flap in the counter, stepped carefully over the sleeping Jones, and grabbed a bottle of Napoleon brandy. 'Like I said, Nick, drinks on the house. Catch hold.'

He passed the bottle across the counter to Holt and fished up two tumblers. 'Fill 'em up, chum.'

Holt did so. He put the bottle down on the counter. The counter began to tilt steeply and the bottle went sliding away, crashed to the floor and broke.

'Careless,' Grade said. He lifted his glass and drank.

Holt was just about to do the same, but staggered as the ship performed one more of its wild dances. He just managed to save himself from falling by clutching at the counter, but half the brandy slopped out of the glass.

'Come back behind the bar,' Grade said. 'It's safer.'

Holt went behind the bar and Grade found another bottle of brandy. They sat down, wedged in with the snoring steward, and began some serious drinking.

Holt was not sure how long they had been there. He was not sure of anything any more, except that warm feeling inside. There was a hellish clatter going on all around, and Grade had been sick more than once over the steward. The steward had stirred a little in his sleep and had muttered something that sounded very much like 'Very much obliged indeed, kind sir,' but he had not opened his eyes. He continued to snore gently.

And then suddenly the bar seemed to be going down, and all the chairs came sliding towards it, sliding down the ever-increasing slope of the floor. There was a tremendous rattling and clinking of glass, and a series of violent shudders were passing through the ship; and still the slope became steeper and steeper. Holt looked up and the world seemed to revolve dizzily overhead. He thought hazily: This is it, this is the big one; this is the one that brings down the curtain. But he was not worrying terribly, because there was that warm feeling inside, and he was really very, very tired; so perhaps it was all for the best.

'Here we go, Tom,' he said. But Grade was not listening. He was being sick again over the steward. This time the steward said nothing; he just went on snoring.

The ship groaned. This was surely the agony of death. She lay over on her side and could not right herself. And then there was a sound like a river in spate; it was a hungry, devouring, engulfing sound; the sound of vast quantities of water, uncontrolled and uncontrollable. This water burst upon the ship and swept over her. She lay under the weight of it and could not rise. She groaned with the straining effort to right herself and could not do so. She was helpless, beaten, buffeted into submission.

It seemed to Holt that the ship stayed like this for a long time. The lights flickered, went out, came on again. And still there was that sound of rushing water; and still the ship lay over on her side and groaned, giving spasmodic jerking movements like the convulsions of a mortally wounded man.

Holt felt an almost detached interest in what was going on. He tried to estimate the angle of list. Forty-five degrees? Fifty? He wondered how securely the bar was fixed to the deck, whether it might tear itself adrift and come down on top of them. He wondered whether the steward was having pleasant dreams.

The ship trembled. The trembling ran through her like a ripple of fear. Then, slowly, painfully, she began to right herself.

Grade still had the bottle in his hand. He drank from the bottle.

★ ★ ★

Captain Leach felt like a man who had been beaten all over with a heavy bludgeon. When he struggled out on to the wing of the bridge the wind caught him and slammed him back against the wheelhouse. Leach slid down to his knees as though praying, then on to all fours. It was the only way; he could not stand against the wind.

Leach was surprised that the *Chetwynd* was still afloat. The great wave that had laid her almost on her beam-ends had washed completely over the wheelhouse, and some of the water had gushed in through one doorway and out through the other. Leach, Prior and the helmsman with the cut face had been thrown down and battered against the wooden side like swimmers caught by a breaker on the beach. It had seemed a very long time indeed before the ship had righted herself and Leach had been able to free his limbs from those of Prior and the helmsman, with which they had become intricately entangled.

'I must go and investigate the damage, Mr. Prior.'

Not that there was much that he could do about it. The odds seemed heavily weighted against the ship's survival now. But Leach knew that many ships had been known to survive against all the odds. You had only to remember the *San Demetrio* and the *Ohio* and countless others. Nevertheless, there could be no blinking the fact that things looked bad.

Still crawling on hands and knees, he came to the opening where the ladder led down from the bridge to the boat-deck. He peered through the opening and a flicker of lightning revealed in a brief, blinding revelation the havoc below him. The boats had all gone, leaving only the twisted davits, the broken rails, the tangled ropes, as a reminder that

246

they had once been there. It was as though a great broom had swept the deck clear of every movable object, leaving it now strangely bare and deserted.

Leach could not be certain, but he feared that the engine-room skylights must have been smashed. Water would probably have gone down into the engine-room. He thought momentarily of Henderson, Henderson's problems. Nothing he could do about them. He had his own problems; too many of them.

He was about to crawl back into the wheelhouse when it occurred to him that it was not quite as dark as it had been. He tried to remember what time it was and came to the conclusion that it must be morning. A new day was dawning, and had it not been for that thick black canopy of cloud, the sun might be shining. The sun! He wondered whether he would ever see it again.

And then, turning his head, he noticed that away on the starboard beam, towards the distant horizon, the sky was most certainly lightening. Could it be that the willy-willy, moving southward along its path of destruction, was leaving the *Chetwynd* behind? He scarcely dared to hope as much, but it was possible, it was just possible.

As though to taunt him for even allowing such faint hopes to creep into his mind, the wind seemed suddenly to increase in ferocity. Leach heard a screeching, cracking sound that could have been metal breaking at last under intolerable strain. Something tall and black, blacker even than the surrounding gloom, was swaying from side to side like a tempest-stricken tree, and he saw with horror that it was the funnel.

He could not move; he could only crouch there and watch it in fascination. It might have been only a few seconds, but it seemed an age. Then the funnel began to topple.

It was a tall, thin funnel, and it fell towards the bridge. Still Leach did not, could not, move. The funnel came down like a falling tower, crashing on the bridge structure. Leach felt the boards under him shudder under the impact, but he was untouched. He began to creep back towards the wheelhouse.

★ ★ ★

Maggs was in the wireless cabin. He had made contact with other ships and shore stations. He hoped that the *Chetwynd* would still be afloat when help arrived, but he was doubtful. He gave the *Chetwynd*'s estimated position and he also reported the murder of Johansen. He had done all that he could. He tried not to let his mind dwell on the fact that it was his fault that the present hazardous situation had arisen.

He did not hear the funnel falling. He heard it strike the roof of the wireless cabin. He heard the woodwork splintering. But he heard these sounds only for a moment before he was crushed beneath the weight of metal and timber.

# 12

## Two of Them

The *Chetwynd* rolled towards Fremantle at the heels of a sea-going tug. Between them the long tow-rope slackened and tautened, dipped under water at the middle and came up dripping.

She was like a ship coming back from a graveyard of ships. There was not a part of her that did not show its record of the storm, did not exhibit its wounds, the evidence of conflict with sea and wind.

There were no boats. The davits were bent and twisted, a block hanging loose here, a fall entangled there. Parts of the rails had gone completely, wrenched off at deck level; others were flattened as though a steam-roller had crashed through them. Derrick booms had been torn from their cradles and thrown athwartships, wreaking more havoc; winches had been uprooted, and there were jagged gaps in the bulwarks. But, strangest sight of all, that which most caught the eye, was the funnel, broken at the root and lying with its top deeply embedded in the shattered wireless cabin.

Mr. Prior and the helmsman had had a lucky escape. The main weight of the funnel had been taken by the wireless cabin, and though the roof of the chartroom and wheelhouse had broken, and though the ironwork of the funnel had come partly through, it had not reached the two men.

The *Chetwynd* was heavy and sluggish at the end of the tow-rope, like an overladen barge. She wallowed, floundered; she had a list to port and was low in the water; she looked a wreck but she floated. She had taken all that the elements could throw at her and she had survived.

★ ★ ★

Mr. Finch, making his way to Captain Leach's cabin, thought how strangely quiet the ship was. No engine pulse, no groaning under the impact of wind and sea. There was no wind; the sea was calm. Finch was feeling happy, because he had expected to die and was still alive. Johansen was dead; Maggs was dead; Major Lycett was presumed dead, since he could not be found; but he, Finch, had escaped. That was something to feel elated about.

He tapped on Captain Leach's door. There

was no answer. He turned the knob and went in.

Leach was lying on the settee, asleep and snoring. There was a whisky bottle on the floor and a broken glass that had apparently dropped from Leach's hand when he had fallen asleep. Some whisky had soaked into the carpet and the reek of it was in the air.

Finch looked at Leach but did not attempt to waken him. What was the use? He thought that perhaps the ordeal they had all passed through and had miraculously survived might have changed things; that Leach might have stayed sober at least until they reached Fremantle. He saw that this was not to be. Nothing had changed, nothing.

But no; he was wrong. Something had changed. For him, Finch, a whole way of life. For he had come to a decision: he would leave the sea. At the very first opportunity he would fly back to Hong Kong and take Ah Mai from that house. He would marry her, get a shore job. It would work out; he would make it work out.

Mr. Finch left the captain's cabin, closed the door gently behind him and walked away, humming a little tune. Happy.

★   ★   ★

Saul and Sara Menstein were also feeling happy, though in a rather more subdued way than Mr. Finch. Menstein felt that he had passed some kind of test by crossing the afterdeck in the storm and facing that wild-eyed man with the knife. The man was progressing satisfactorily, thanks to the doctor's attention, and Finch and Holt had both praised the courage which Menstein had shown. Everyone in the ship knew about it, and Menstein, rather to his embarrassment, found himself quite a hero.

'I am not really so brave, you know, Sara,' he confided to his wife. 'I was very much afraid.'

Sara patted his arm affectionately. 'But that is true courage. I am proud of you, Saul.'

He smiled at her. 'If you are proud of me, who bothers about other people?'

★ ★ ★

Two detectives had come out with the tug to investigate the murder of Carl Johansen. They were of the opinion, after interviewing everyone who could throw any light on the matter, that it was an open and shut case. The fact that Lycett could not be found pointed to his guilt. Having killed Johansen in a mad fit of rage and jealousy, he had probably

253

thrown himself overboard; it was not at all unusual for a murderer to commit suicide. Their failure to discover any murder weapon did not bother them greatly; no doubt Lycett had carried it away and taken it into the sea with him. There would be an inquest, of course, but it looked as though any sort of trial was entirely ruled out.

It took the Chetwynd and tug four days to reach Fremantle. On the day they made port Holt invited Sydney East to come to his cabin. He knew that Grade was on deck and that they would not be disturbed.

'I'd like to have a little talk,' Holt said.

East looked at him in surprise. 'What do you want to talk about?'

'Oh, just a certain matter that needs clearing up. And I've got something to give you.'

'Something to give me?' East looked startled. Holt thought he looked rather ill too; there were dark pouches under his eyes, as though he had been sleeping badly.

'Just a small memento of an eventful voyage.'

Holt led the way into the cabin with East following, a shade reluctantly. They went inside. Holt closed the door.

'You don't look too well.' he said.

East answered rather petulantly, 'I'm all

254

right. Now what do you want to talk to me about?'

Holt walked to the open porthole and looked out. He could see the steelwork of a crane on the quay, a large open shed beyond it.

He said without turning, 'Why did you kill Johansen?'

East did not answer. There was a small scuffling sound, as though perhaps he had made a movement forward — or back. That was all.

Holt turned. East was standing with his back pressed against the door. He looked older. Was it a trick of the light, or was his face more lined, his hair greyer?

'You did kill him, of course.' It was a statement, not a question.

'How — ?' East said, then stopped.

'How did I know?' Holt put a hand in his pocket and pulled out the small, silvery object that he had found beside Johansen's body. He let it rest in the palm of his hand, holding it out to the other man. 'This is yours, isn't it?'

It was a shirt button of rather unusual appearance, square, not round. Holt had seen East wearing a shirt with buttons like that. He had never seen any others quite like them.

East made no move to take the button. He said in a hoarse voice, as though his throat was dry, 'Where did you get it?'

'I think you know,' Holt said. 'I think you've guessed.'

'What are you going to do?'

Holt repeated his earlier question. 'Why did you kill him?'

East put out a hand like a blind man groping his way, found the chair and sat down. 'It was an accident.'

Holt sat on the lower bunk, facing him. 'I don't think that's quite good enough. There was a fight. It was obvious from the state of the cabin. You don't fight a man by accident.'

'Not that,' East said. 'That wasn't the accident. Of course I had a fight with him. I was going to teach him a lesson. But I never intended to kill him.'

'Why did you want to teach him a lesson?'

'He assaulted my wife.' East's eyes blazed for a moment. 'The damned filthy swine. I'm not sorry he's dead; he deserved to die. But I didn't mean to kill him.'

Holt was not surprised. He had guessed that it was something of the kind. He had seen the mate's eyes when he looked at Pearl East. Johansen had never taken any pains to hide his admiration for a pretty woman, or his desire.

'He got her into his cabin by offering to lend her some books. Then he tried to make love to her. When she resisted he knocked her out.'

Holt could understand East's feeling. He must have been in a fury when he heard what had happened. No doubt he had rushed straight to the mate's cabin.

'What did you do with the weapon?'

'I didn't have any weapon. Just my bare hands.'

'But the gash in Johansen's forehead — '

'I told you. It was an accident. We were struggling, and you know how the ship was rolling. He fell, hit his head on the ironwork of the bunk. I thought at first he was just stunned. Then I knew he was dead.'

'And you were going to let Major Lycett take the rap?'

East shook his head violently. 'No, no, no. Not if he'd still been alive. I'd have come forward. But when I heard he couldn't be found it seemed like an act of providence. And there was Pearl to consider; I had to think of her. Lycett is dead. What harm can it do him?'

'Mrs. Lycett is still alive.'

'I know. I've thought of that. But will it really hurt her? The inquest may just come up with a verdict of murder by person or persons unknown. That sort of thing. The police can't charge a man who's dead, can they?'

There was something in that. Whatever happened, Lycett would not be troubled. And Mrs. Lycett? She would get over it.

Holt noticed that East was looking at him, worried. 'Are you going to tell the police.'

'I've left it a bit late for that, haven't I? They might want to know why I didn't say anything about the button at once. Suppression of evidence is a crime, you know.' He reached across, grasped East's right hand and pressed the button into it. 'I never saw that thing in Johansen's cabin. For all I know, it's still sewn on your shirt.'

East seemed to be trying to say something without making any success of it.

'Forget it,' Holt said. 'I like the act.'

★ ★ ★

She was waiting for him in the cabin when he went in.

'Nick Holt knows,' he said.

She looked dismayed. 'Oh, no, Syd, no.'

He reassured her quickly. 'It's all right. He's not going to say anything.' He showed her the button. 'He found this. He said for all he knows it's still sewn on my shirt.'

'But why? Why should he do this — for us?'

East gave a wry smile. 'He says he likes the act.'

258

She began to cry, covering her face with her hands.

He put his arm round her shoulders. 'Ah, now, honey, now. It'll be all right. Everything will be fine.'

He held her for a little while, waiting for the sobbing to pass. Then he said, 'It's funny in a way. Because there isn't going to be an act any more.'

She stared at him. 'No act?'

'I'm not going to fool myself any longer,' he said. 'I'm going to do what you want me to do. I'm going to get a job.'

★　★　★

He was a tall, slightly stooping man with black hair and a nose like an ancient Roman. He looked about forty and he was expensively dressed.

'My name's Roylance,' he said. 'You're Nick Holt, aren't you?' He spoke with an unmistakable Australian accent and when he shook hands his grip was strong and bony. 'That all your luggage? Give me one of the bags. I've got a car.'

The car was a Jaguar. Roylance drove with nonchalant skill. Holt noticed a black car behind. He wondered whether it was following. Roylance appeared not to notice it.

'I've booked rooms at an hotel,' he said. 'Got some business in Fremantle tomorrow. That suit you?'

'Anything suits me,' Holt said. It was only twelve miles to Perth; the Jaguar could have made it in fifteen minutes maybe. But he did not remark on this. If Mr. Roylance wanted to put up at a Fremantle hotel, that was his business.

It was in a quiet street away from the waterfront. Everything about the hotel seemed quiet. Perhaps that was how Roylance liked it. There was a quiet lobby, quiet stairs, a quiet room with a view of trees. The trees were quiet too; there was no wind.

'I think you'll be comfortable here for the night,' Roylance said. 'I've got the next room.'

He crossed to the window and looked out at the quiet trees. Then, casually, 'Did you bring something for me?'

'Oh, yes,' Holt said, as though for the moment it had slipped his memory. 'A box of China tea.'

He put one of the suitcases on the bed and opened it. He took out the plywood box. When he looked up he saw that Roylance had moved to the bed.

'China tea is one of my vices.'

'A small vice, Mr. Roylance.'

Roylance chuckled. 'As you say, a small vice.'

He took the box from Holt. He had it in his hands when the plain-clothes men came in. The way they handled Roylance made Holt feel thankful that he had decided to put himself on the right side of the law. If Mr. Saunders ever set foot in Australia again no doubt they would handle him in much the same way.

★  ★  ★

Grade was in a bar drinking beer. Grade considered that he had had a raw deal. First there had been Lycett; he had spent half the voyage getting the major nicely hooked, feeding him that stuff about an uncle with interests in nickel mines; and then, before he could even complete the con, Lycett had had to go and kill Johansen and throw himself overboard. Downright upsporting of him, in Grade's opinion. And if that were not enough, there was Nick Holt coming over all moral and law-abiding when they could have split forty thousand dollars between them. Hell, it made you want to spit, too true, it did.

He drained his glass, put it down on the bar. 'Gimme another.'

He looked in his wallet. Ten dollars. Ten lousy Australian dollars. How far could you go on that, for Pete's sake? He paid for the beer and took a long, cool drink. There was only one thing for it: he would have to look for another sucker. There was one born every minute.

★ ★ ★

Leach was also drinking — alone, in his cabin. He knew that the *Chetwynd* was finished. The owners would never consider her worth the money it would take to make her sea-worthy again. They would sell her to some ship-breaker for what they could get. She had had a long life but now she was near the end of it; she had fought her last fight with the old enemy, the sea.

Leach raised his glass, looked at the whisky. And what about him? Where did he go from here? To another Barling-Orient ship? Always supposing there was one for him. What did it matter? What in hell did it matter?

He drank the whisky, put the glass down, rammed his cap on his head and walked out of the cabin. He climbed up to the bridge and looked at his battered ship. So still she was now, so quiet. Difficult to cast one's mind back to that night when he had had to crawl on hands and knees because of the fury of the wind. He had thought it was the end then, but he was still alive. And for what purpose? What point was there to it all when you came down to it? What point?

He saw someone walking down the gangway to the quay. A woman. Mrs. Lycett. He thought she looked lonely, stepping slowly, uncertainly, as though she did not know where to go. Lonely; so terribly lonely.

He turned away with a muttered curse. Well, that made two of them.

DEAD OF WINTER
SPECIAL DELIVERY
SKELETON ISLAND
BUSMAN'S HOLIDAY
A PASSAGE OF ARMS
ON DESPERATE SEAS
THE SPAYDE CONSPIRACY
CRANE
OLD PALS ACT
THE SILENT VOYAGE
THE ANGRY ISLAND
SOMETHING OF VALUE
THE GOLDEN REEF
BULLION

We do hope that you have enjoyed reading this large print book.

Did you know that all of our titles are available for purchase?

We publish a wide range of high quality large print books including:
**Romances, Mysteries, Classics General Fiction Non Fiction and Westerns**

Special interest titles available in large print are:
**The Little Oxford Dictionary Music Book Song Book Hymn Book Service Book**

Also available from us courtesy of Oxford University Press:
**Young Readers' Dictionary (large print edition) Young Readers' Thesaurus (large print edition)**

For further information or a free brochure, please contact us at:
**Ulverscroft Large Print Books Ltd., The Green, Bradgate Road, Anstey, Leicester, LE7 7FU, England. Tel:** (00 44) 0116 236 4325
**Fax:** (00 44) 0116 234 0205

*Other titles published by*
*The House of Ulverscroft:*

## BULLION

### James Pattinson

Alan Caley was far from delighted to receive a phone call from his old school pal Chuck Brogan, suggesting that the two of them should get together for lunch. It was quite some time since he had last seen Brogan — the man had been sent to prison for a number of years for taking part in a bullion robbery. Caley felt inclined to refuse the invitation, but Brogan hinted that the meeting might be to Caley's advantage — financially. And Caley could surely use some help in that respect. So he agreed to have lunch with Brogan, little suspecting what dire consequences were to stem from that free meal.

# THE GOLDEN REEF

## James Pattinson

When the S.S. *Southern Queen* encountered a lifeboat in the Pacific Ocean, a strange mystery was uncovered. For the lifeboat was marked *Valparaiso I* and the *Valparaiso* had been sunk by a Japanese submarine in January 1945, nearly a year earlier. Moreover, the *Valparaiso* had been carrying a million pounds' worth of gold bullion. There was a man in the lifeboat, but his memory had gone — or so he claimed. When he showed an unaccountable desire some years later to return to the Pacific, two other survivors from the *Valparaiso* decided to keep on eye on him, because a million pounds in gold bullion is worth anybody's time and, if necessary, more than a little violence.

# THE ANGRY ISLAND

## James Pattinson

When Guy Radford goes to visit an old college friend on the West Indian island of St Marien, he is blissfully unaware of the trouble he is flying into. Divisions of race and wealth have created such tensions between desperate workers and powerful plantation owners that a violent show-down is inevitable. When Radford unwittingly becomes caught in the cross-fire, he finds his own life in danger. And, as the conflict intensifies, the fact that he has fallen in love adds merely one more complication to an already tricky situation . . .

# THE SILENT VOYAGE

## James Pattinson

World War Two has ended a few years earlier and the Cold War is starting when Brett Manning is sent to do some business in Archangel. But on his way, in the thick fog and darkness of the Barents Sea, his ship is run down by a much larger vessel. Only Brett and one other man are picked up, and they now find themselves on board a Russian freighter bound for a secret destination. Slowly it dawns on Brett and his companion that they now know too much for their own good and that their very lives are in danger. But how does one escape from a ship at sea?

# CRANE

## James Pattinson

Paul Crane had not altogether liked the look of Skene and West when they turned up at his north Norfolk cottage and made him an offer he could not refuse, but his chequered past had taught him not to be particular. Down on his luck since eighteen, when he was picked up on Liverpool Street Station by the decidedly odd Heathcliff, Crane promptly teamed up with a young thief named Charlie Green. Only when he fell in love with Penelope was there any hope of going straight. And perhaps he would have stuck to his promise if the chance of making a million had not dropped into his lap.

# OLD PALS ACT

## James Pattinson

Steve Brady had not seen Linda Manning for years. Then, out of the blue, she turned up on his doorstep. They had worked together, off and on, when she had been working for British Intelligence. Now she was in quite a different kind of job; though, in fact, he was to discover that there were similarities. She wanted him to join forces with her once again. There was to be no risk to life or limb — but he had heard that one before. And down in South America you never knew what might turn up. Dead bodies were only part of it . . .